Princess
of the Six
Flowers

KONOSUBA:
GOD'S BLESSING ON THIS
WONDERFUL WORLD
6!

"I shall surprise and astonish Her Royal Highness with a spectacular entrance such as only the Crimson Magic Clan can perform."

Megumin

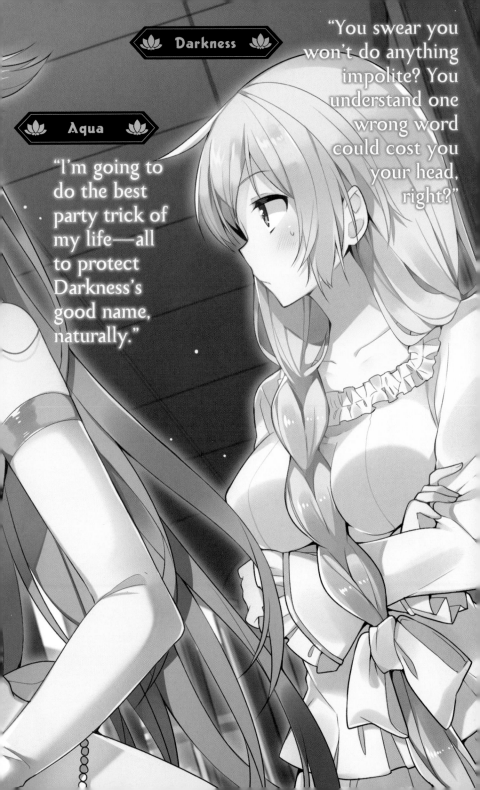

Darkness

"You swear you won't do anything impolite? You understand one wrong word could cost you your head, right?"

Aqua

"I'm going to do the best party trick of my life—all to protect Darkness's good name, naturally."

"I've never
met anyone
like you
before."

Eris

"I can't help admiring that righteous thief a little bit."

KONOSUBA: GOD'S BLESSING ON THIS WONDERFUL WORLD! 6

Princess of the Six Flowers

CONTENTS

KONOSUBA: GOD'S BLESSING ON THIS WONDERFUL WORLD!

Princess of the Six Flowers

6

NATSUME AKATSUKI

ILLUSTRATION BY
KURONE MISHIMA

YEN
ON
NEW YORK

KONOSUBA: GOD'S BLESSING ON THIS WONDERFUL WORLD! 6

NATSUME AKATSUKI

Translation by Kevin Steinbach
Cover art by Kurone Mishima

KONO SUBARASHII SEKAI NI SHUKUFUKU WO!, Volume 6: ROKKA NO OUJO
Copyright © 2015 Natsume Akatsuki, Kurone Mishima
First published in Japan in 2015 by KADOKAWA CORPORATION, Tokyo.
English translation rights arranged with KADOKAWA CORPORATION, Tokyo, through TUTTLE-MORI AGENCY, INC., Tokyo.

English translation © 2018 by Yen Press, LLC

Yen On
1290 Avenue of the Americas
New York, NY 10104

Visit us at yenpress.com
facebook.com/yenpress
twitter.com/yenpress
yenpress.tumblr.com
instagram.com/yenpress

First Yen On Edition: August 2018

Yen On is an imprint of Yen Press, LLC.
The Yen On name and logo are trademarks of Yen Press, LLC.

The publisher is not responsible for websites (or their content) that are not owned by the publisher.

Library of Congress Cataloging-in-Publication Data
Names: Akatsuki, Natsume, author. | Mishima, Kurone, 1991– illustrator. | Steinbach, Kevin, translator.
Title: Konosuba, God's blessing on this wonderful world! / Natsume Akatsuki ; illustration by Kurone Mishima ; translation by Kevin Steinbach.
Other titles: Kono subarashi sekai ni shukufuku wo. English
Description: First Yen On edition. | New York, NY : Yen On, 2017–
Identifiers: LCCN 2016052009 | ISBN 9780316553377 (v. 1 : paperback) |
    ISBN 9780316468701 (v. 2 : paperback) | ISBN 9780316468732 (v. 3 : paperback) |
    ISBN 9780316468763 (v. 4 : paperback) | ISBN 9780316468787 (v. 5 : paperback) |
    ISBN 9780316468800 (v. 6 : paperback)
Subjects: | CYAC: Fantasy. | Future life—Fiction. | Adventure and adventurers—Fiction. |
    BISAC: FICTION / Fantasy / General.
Classification: LCC PZ7.1.A38 Ko 2017 | DDC [Fic]—dc23
LC record available at https://lccn.loc.gov/2016052009

ISBNs: 978-0-316-46880-0 (paperback)
    978-0-316-46881-7 (ebook)

10 9 8 7 6 5 4 3

LSC-C

Printed in the United States of America

KONOSUBA: GOD'S BLESSING ON THIS WONDERFUL WORLD!

Princess of the Six Flowers

Characters

Darkness

Age 18
Job Crusader

A female knight who specializes in defense and enjoys being beaten up by monsters. Daughter of the Dustiness family, a powerful noble house. Special skill: fantasizing.

Aqua

Age Unknown
Job Arch-priest

A goddess who gives guidance to the young and deceased. Goes to a parallel world with Kazuma to defeat the Demon King. Likes wine. Special skill: party tricks.

Megumin

Age 14
Job Arch-wizard

Exceptionally talented, even by Crimson Magic Clan standards. Obsessed with the überpowerful spell Explosion, she is neither capable of nor interested in using any other magic. Favorite thing: Explosion. Special skill: Explosion. Hobby: Explosion.

Iris

Age 12
Job Princess

Wiz

Age 20
Job Shopkeeper

Kazuma Satou

Age 16
Job Adventurer

An adventurer and *hikikomori* (in any world) who brought Aqua to their current plane. Has already given up on defeating the Demon King.

Chris

Age 15?
Job Thief

Vanir

Age Unknown
Job Terrible Demon, Shopkeeper

When I opened my eyes, I didn't even bother getting out of the soft bed. I just clapped my hands, summoning the butler who stood near the door. A white-haired old man in a perfectly tailored suit responded to the sound.

He gave a deep bow of his head. "You called, Master Kazuma?"

"Yeah. I'd like my morning coffee, Sebastian."

"I'm Heidel."

"I'd like my morning coffee, Heidel."

Then I lay back down on the bed. Eventually the maid, Mary, would come to change the sheets. But I wouldn't make it easy on her. I had all kinds of ways of tripping her up as she tried to work. A certain Crusader somewhere had told me that was the proper way to behave toward maids.

Finally, a knock came at the door.

See? Called it.

It must be my personal maid, Mary...

Chapter 1

May We Celebrate This Bright Future!

1

After so much traveling, there was no place like home—even if it was neglected and covered in dust. I was sitting cross-legged on the carpet in the middle of our living room, thinking back on everything that had happened recently.

A certain girl we knew had gotten a letter saying that Crimson Magic Village, a veritable holy city for Arch-wizards and the source of so many talented magic-users, was under attack by the army of the Demon King.

Even knowing she would be of little help alone, the girl nonetheless resolved to go back to her village. She knew she might never return to Axel—and so she confessed to me what she had kept hidden in her heart all this time: that she wanted to be loved before she went off to die.

I turned her down flat and set off on a journey, leaving the heart-broken girl behind. Yes: I would not allow her to risk herself. I would destroy the Demon King's army instead.

Well, what with this and that, I defeated Sylvia, the Demon King's general, and peace returned once more to Crimson Magic Village...

"...Kazuma, the way you've just been sitting there grinning is really starting to weird me out. I guess maybe that's what happens when the weather gets warmer like this."

I had been living a tranquil existence ever since we returned to town. Aqua—the one making the smart remarks—was sitting on the couch beside Darkness and Megumin. They were all taking turns at the portable game Aqua had brought back from Crimson Magic Village.

I suddenly snapped back to reality. I turned to the three of them and, in my most serious tone, informed them:

"I want a little sister."

That shut them all up, if only for a second. But then…

"Hey, Darkness, we have to take turns. I'm next, okay? I want to be the one who beats the last boss."

"Aww, come on, you and Megumin are the ones who always beat the bosses in real life. Can't I at least do it in this game?"

"No. As a member of the Crimson Magic Clan, I cannot allow another to strike the final blow. And anyway, the last boss is always the most powerful enemy. The way you just charge in, Darkness, we would be lucky to beat him if we used all our continues."

They went on bickering. Apparently, they had collectively decided to ignore me.

"Will you listen to me?!"

"Waaah! Stop it! We've almost beaten the game! We all worked really hard to get this far!"

Even as I dodged Aqua's attempts to snatch back the game I had taken from her, I played it myself, until…

"There, last boss done. I didn't even take any damage. Are you happy now?!"

"Not at all! Why do *you* get to do the best part?! We spent three days getting that far!"

"Whatever! Let me have it, then. In three hours I'll get you back to where you were, and I'll do it without taking a hit!"

"Stop! Please stop making our best efforts look so bad…" Aqua, half weeping, grabbed the game back.

"And to think I was almost impressed by what you did in Crimson Magic Village!" Darkness said. "I should have known you were still just a rat! Do you enjoy making all our work go to waste?! Come on, Megumin, tell him!"

"…Why ostracize Kazuma?" Megumin asked the enraged Darkness. "In Crimson Magic Village, he was really the one who saved us in the end, as he often is. This just now was very characteristic of our party, and I rather like that."

""Huh?!"" Aqua and Darkness looked at Megumin and me in shock.

"Are you feeling all right, Megumin?" Aqua asked. "You're usually quicker than anyone to complain about Kazuma. What happened to the most notoriously argumentative wizard in Axel?"

"She's right," Darkness said. "Everyone agrees our impulsive Megumin is more suited than anyone else to the advanced front-row class of Berserker; there's no way she would say something so measured and adult. Hey, Kazuma, what exactly happened in Crimson Magic Village?"

"I cannot believe either of you! I am an Arch-wizard, a class renowned for their calm rationality! …Anyway, Kazuma, what is this sudden request? If you want a little sister, I must imagine it would do more good to tell your parents than us."

"I did tell them, a bunch of times. In fact, I told them I wanted a little stepsister, so they ought to get divorced and remarry someone with a kid. Come to think of it, that might be the first time one of my parents ever slapped me…"

"Your parents must have been wonderful people to not chase you out of the house for saying something like that."

"Forget about them! I can't go back home anyway, so what does it matter? I have something more important in mind." I didn't think they were following me. I gave a theatrical shake of my head. "I have the comforting older woman Wiz. The energetic, eager young lady Chris. Sena's the 'cool' type. And there's the sweet but luckless Yunyun! I even have Lady Eris, the royal heroine. In other words, I've met beautiful women and girls from practically every archetype!"

"Ooh, what about me, Kazuma? What beautiful-woman archetype am I?"

"None of them. You're not a potential romantic interest. You're more of a pet— H-hey! I'm trying to be serious here, so save it for later!" I brushed Aqua aside as she charged at me with a balled-up fist. "My point is, I've noticed something really important. I'm still missing a certain archetype! Back home in Japan, I even had a childhood friend, more or less. I'm sure you can tell what's missing, right?"

Megumin seemed to have caught on, because she sighed deeply. "I believe I see where this is going…," she said. "Put simply, you want me to fill the little-sister role, correct?"

"What? No, you're my jailbait."

"Wh-what?!" She seemed surprised for some reason. Beside her, an embarrassed-looking Darkness hesitantly raised her hand.

"S-so what c-category does that put me in…?"

"You're the lewd one, obviously."

"Lewd one?!" She seemed as shocked as Megumin. I decided to try to wrap up the discussion.

"Okay, remember when we went to Crimson Magic Village? Remember Megumin's little sister? She got me thinking again about how much I want one of my own. So you understand what I'm saying now, right?"

Aqua, who had been listening intently to the entire conversation, replied:

"Not one bit."

There was a perfectly good reason I was bringing this up now. And that was…

"A princess, huh? I hear she's younger than me. Maybe she's the little-sister character…"

That's right: This had to do with my hopes for the princess, who had written me a letter. I'd heard talk that put her at about twelve years old. That was obviously too young for me, but maybe we could at least be friends, and she would call me *Big Brother* and everything.

Darkness may or may not have had any idea I felt this way, but ever since we had gotten back from Crimson Magic Village, she had periodically tried to dissuade me.

"…Come on, Kazuma. It's not too late—let's turn her down! You know? We're talking about the number one family in the whole country, here. I guarantee what you think of as a nice dinner won't be anything like what they're planning. It'll be all formal and stuff! You know? Hey, everybody, let's pretend this never happened!"

The past few days, she had tried everything to stop us from meeting with the princess. The tone she was taking suggested she was even more desperate than usual this time.

Still sitting on the carpet, I muttered, "…You're afraid I'll be rude to the princess, aren't you?"

That made Darkness twitch. She looked around the room for a moment, then finally lowered her head.

"That's… That's not it at all… Really."

Yeah, sure.

"Hey, look at me when you're talking and drop the facade. You're worried we'll get out of line and do something to harm the Dustiness name."

"You are?! Darkness, how cruel! I do know how to behave in polite company!"

"This is a great shock! Darkness, what makes you think we would ever do something to cause trouble for you? Are we not comrades in arms? You should trust us more!"

Aqua and Megumin were quick to respond to my accusation.

"Er…argh… Honestly? It's exactly because I know you better than anyone that I'm so worried…," Darkness said, near tears. She looked absolutely terrified.

"I know the princess is way above me, and I've got at least the basics of etiquette down. I'm just a little worked up because I'm meeting such a refined young lady. That's all."

"H-hey! You've already met me! I'm a refined young lady, you'll remember!" Even when she looked like she was about to start crying, Darkness was able to snap at me.

This constant worrying was a side of Darkness I'd never seen before.

"Oops, guess I'd better buy a tuxedo. And you two, you don't have any dresses, do you? I think this calls for a trip to the tailor." I was really starting to get into this. And Aqua and Megumin didn't seem the least bit interested in backing out.

"Great idea!" Aqua said. "I do like wearing something other than this feather mantle every once in a while. But is there enough time to have clothes made?"

"My dress will be black, of course. One that simply oozes maturity."

Darkness, looking closer to weeping than ever, said, "Y-you guys…! We're talking about the princess of the entire country, all right? You could literally be putting your lives on the line! Tell them, Kazuma!"

"Ah, but everyone wears a tuxedo. I need something that'll really leave an impression on her. I know! A kimono and *hakama*!"

"Please, I'm begging you! If it's in my power, I'll do anything you ask, just don't show up in some bizarre outfit!"

Darkness was clearly at the end of her rope.

2

"All right, you said 'anything.' So for the week until the princess gets here, I'm gonna put you to work."

It was the day after Darkness had made her impassioned plea.

"…F-fine. So you weren't kidding back in Crimson Magic Village. I see I've underestimated you again."

She was dressed in a maid outfit, one deliberately a bit too small. The short skirt lent her an eroticism perfectly suited to our resident hottie. She stood in front of me now, looking defeated. I couldn't help but get a little carried away at the sight of her.

"I think what you mean is *I understand, Master!*"

"Hrm…hrrgh! I—I understand, Master! I am a lowly swine…!!"

"Hey, I didn't tell you to say that."

Darkness was red and trembling.

In exchange for giving up my kimono idea, and on the condition that I completely behave myself around the princess, I was finally able to realize my long-held dream. Yes: the one where I put Darkness in a skimpy maid outfit and force her to tend to my every whim.

Admittedly, I didn't indulge quite *everything* I could think of, because I was afraid of what she might do to me later if I got too full of myself. But it's fine to claim a few perks every once in a while…

"What should I do, then? I've never actually done housework before. I have no idea what to do. I guess, for starters, I could spill tea on the crotch of your pants and then frantically try to wipe it up. Would that work?"

"You are definitely not allowed to make tea." What exactly did she think a maid's job was? "Just, you know, start cleaning or something. But not the dishes. You'll just break them. I can't afford a maid like that."

"…Hmm. All right…" She seemed disappointed as she trudged out of the living room.

Aqua and Megumin were at Wiz's shop. Which meant it was just Darkness and me in this huge house.

Come to think of it, Darkness really caused me nothing but trouble. I would have to work her like a dog today.

But then…

"Eeeeeeeek!"

What sounded like a pretend scream was followed by the crash of breaking pottery. Then Darkness came running in, clutching a fragment of something.

"I am so sorry, Master! I broke your precious vase! Please punish me *however* you see fit…!"

"I don't have a precious vase. I don't think I have any vases at all. And if you break anything that really is important to me, I'll punish you by making you go to the Adventurer's Guild in that outfit."

"?!"

Darkness was attacking the housework, running a cloth along the windowsills, ignoring the fact that she was getting covered in dust. I was checking to see how good a job she was doing. Why? Because I had time to kill.

I ran my finger along the windowsill and looked at it. I had expected it to come away dusty—but instead, it was perfectly clean.

"Grr! You're never good at anything—why now? And I was so looking forward to sending my maid, Crusader Lalatina, to the Guild as punishment…"

"Heh-heh. You won't punish me that easily, even if you do know how to push my buttons. Speaking of which, seriously, please don't call me Lalatina. Please?" I hated to admit it, but the beet-red Darkness got full marks for cleaning.

Not just cleaning, either.

I grumbled as I ate the lunch Darkness had prepared for me per my request.

"…Grr. I thought for sure you'd mix up the salt and the sugar or something…"

"Why would I do that? They're clearly labeled. And as an adventurer, I do know how to cook meat."

She must have figured out I had no real desire to punish her when I picked a simple recipe consisting of rice, meat, and raw vegetables that even she couldn't screw up.

She was wearing a triumphant look on her face. "Heh-heh! I used some pretty high-class meat. How does it taste?"

"Average."

"?!"

Bathroom cleaning:
This was normally Aqua's job.

"Do... Do you really think this toilet needs cleaning...?"

"I guess...maybe not," I said.

I hardly ever saw Aqua actually cleaning, but the toilet sparkled brighter than anything in the house. Leave it to a water goddess, I guess...

Oh well. On to the next thing.

"Really?! Is this really a maid's most important job?! You're not just making that up because you know how sheltered and unworldly I am, are you? I know my father never made the help in our house do this, at least!"

"Yeah? Well, where I come from, a maid who doesn't do this can't call herself a maid!"

I was walking in and out of the front door, and every time I came in, Darkness had to smile and say, *Welcome home, Master.*

"Come on! What a forced smile! How come you're always so cold?! You're practically scaring me! Welcome me back with a smile that lights up the room!"

"W-welcome home, Master!!"

"Wrong! Hands here! Feet here! You know your hotness is your only redeeming quality, so make use of it—lean forward more! Okay, from the top!"

"Welcome home, Master! I do enjoy a certain level of harassment, but overdo it and I'll show you my other redeeming quality—my powerful grip!"

"Yaaaargh! My head! I swear my brains are coming out! I'm sorry!" I bellowed as Darkness dug her iron fingers into my temples.

3

"Sheesh. I might have been willing to play along if you'd punished me or harassed me in a way that was more, you know, *exciting.*"

"Hey, when it looked like we were gonna cross that line, you backed off just like I did." Having teased Darkness to my satisfaction, I went for a stroll with her through town. "You know, that maid outfit looked pretty good on you. You should wear frilly things more often."

Darkness had begged me not to make her go into town in her maid uniform, so I had allowed her to change back into her usual clothes.

"…I know better than anyone that cute clothes don't suit me. Please let me do the housework tomorrow in my regular outfit…"

"Absolutely not."

Darkness hung her head dejectedly, but why did she also look kind of happy? As we talked, we finally arrived at the store I'd set out for.

"Knock knock, anyone home?"

"Oh, Mr. Kazuma, hello! We were just stocking the lighter you came up with."

We had come to Wiz's shop. Today was the day she would start selling a variety of convenient items from Japan. Inside the store we found Megumin, looking at some of my inventions with interest, and Aqua, quietly nursing a piece of candy she'd been given. The most distinctive member of the shop's staff seemed to be absent.

When she saw me come in, Megumin called me over, holding my oil-based lighter.

"Kazuma! Kazuma! Quick! Show me what this magic item does!"

"I keep telling you, it's not magic. It's just a helpful little doodad from my home country. Anyway, here." I took the lighter and lit it.

""""Whoa!!"""""

Megumin, Darkness, and Wiz all gawked at the flame it produced.

"Th-this is great! It's exactly like Kindle! This will sell for sure, Mr. Kazuma!" Wiz was ecstatic.

"It is well made for something so simple. I cannot believe it is not magic. And properly cared for, it seems it could be used for a very long time." Megumin seemed enthralled as she took the lighter and examined it from several angles.

"I want one of those," Darkness said. "Flints are hard to use when it's wet out, it takes time to start a fire, and you have to be careful of your kindling getting damp while you're carrying it. This solves all those problems. Wiz, Kazuma, I'll take one. How much?" She pulled out her wallet.

Wiz smiled. "Oh, don't worry about money. Mr. Kazuma thought of these things, and we manufactured them, and all of you helped develop them. Take whatever you like."

Darkness grinned and picked up a lighter. Watching her and Megumin, Aqua continued to munch on her candy. She gave a mocking little snort and laughed. "What a bunch of primitives! All excited about one little lighter. That thing is simple! I guess this is what you get, dealing with ignorant savages…"

Even as she sneered at Wiz and the others, Aqua's hand reached out toward one of the lighters…

I smacked it away.

"………What? Come on, Kazuma, let me pick something."

"No way. You want an item, pony up. How do you think commerce works?" I added, causing Aqua to lunge at me.

"What?! What's wrong with you?! Why are you always so mean to me?! Wiz said we could each have something! Darkness and Megumin got to pick, so why not me? Am I not one of our party members?"

"I wouldn't have made a big deal about it if you hadn't made fun of them. How, exactly, did you contribute to any of this anyway? Wiz runs the shop, obviously. Megumin showed me how the Crimson Magic Clan makes its magical items. And Darkness introduced me to some wholesalers she knows. And all that time, you were just eating and drinking and sleeping at home. You want a piece of the action? Maybe go find us some customers or something."

Tears welled up in Aqua's eyes. As she fled the store, she shouted:

"Waaaah! Worthless Kazuma! I wasn't even going to tell anyone how I saw you sniffing my dirty laundry the other day!"

"W-wait a second, I never did that! Don't make stuff up! Come back here! …I swear! I never— Megumin, Darkness, don't look at me like— W-Wiz, you too?! It's not truuue!"

As I tried desperately to undo the misunderstanding Aqua had caused, the culprit poked her head back in the doorway of the shop.

"…So if I get a bunch of people to come here, I can pick something?"

"Fine! Just tell these three you were kidding!"

4

There was a massive crowd in front of the magic-item shop. Wiz said she had never seen so many people knocking on her door. The commotion might have been in part because Vanir, who had yet to arrive at the store, was in town passing out flyers. I could see several members of the crowd clutching the leaflets.

"…Gosh. What a crowd."

"No kidding."

As Darkness mumbled to herself, I gave a halfhearted reply.

"…It would be great if they were all here to buy something."

"Sure would."

To Megumin's comment, I offered only a tepid response.

I peered into the crowd. Next to me, Wiz was looking very distraught.

"E-everyone's distracted—even the people who were coming to my store!"

"Gaaaah! What is *wrong* with her?!"

In the middle of the crowd, we could see Aqua, showing off her party tricks and basking in the attention. The crowd included people carrying leaflets, which meant they had probably come to shop. But by now, they had completely forgotten why they were here.

She'd brought in plenty of people—but no customers.

Aqua herself seemed to have forgotten what she was supposed to be doing; she was putting on the best display she could muster.

"For my next trick! Observe this completely ordinary handkerchief! Behold as it transforms into a dove!" She opened the cloth with a flourish.

A classic bit of sleight of hand. You hid a dove in your clothes ahead of time, then you made it look like it was coming out of the handkerchief. But when Aqua waved her handkerchief...

""""Ooooh!""""

...a flock of several hundred doves scattered through the crowd.

"What the hell?! Where'd she get all those birds?! That shouldn't even be physically possible!" I exclaimed, turning to Wiz. I was starting to doubt my own eyes.

"I—I wonder. I didn't sense any magic, so it probably wasn't a summoning spell. But where could she have hidden so many animals? I'm really stumped..." She put a hand over her mouth in amazement. Even our magical expert was flummoxed.

Aqua's audience was practically flinging coins at her, but she said, "Oh, no money, please! I'm not a street performer—please hold your donations!" I guess she was principled when it came to her art. Even if it looked like she could make a living off it.

Half out of annoyance and half out of interest, we waded into the crowd to watch Aqua's performance. That was when we heard a voice.

"Wh-what a sight this is...!"

Vanir had come back, and he was staring at the crowd, dumbfounded.

In the middle of it all, Aqua was standing with a bunch of potions she had presumably gotten from Wiz's store.

"Now! When I count to three, every single one of these potions is going to disappear! Where will they go? Nobody knows! *Including me...* Okay! One! Two...!"

"Don't you dare say *three*, you divine dimwit! What are you doing here?! I see you are not content with splashing holy water on our door-knob every chance you get, and you've taken to diverting our business right in front of our very store!"

I'd always wondered what she'd been up to on all those "little walks."

"Hey, don't interrupt, you masked moron! This is a public road—you can't complain if I do my art here!"

"I most certainly can! Today is the day we put out the new stock on which we've staked the very future of this shop! This should be a day of celebration, and I don't have time to play with people who go out of their way to harm my business!"

Vanir and Aqua forgot about the audience as they bickered, so Wiz raised her voice: "Hello, one and all! Today we offer you a wide variety of convenient items! Please come take a look!"

Wow! It was the first time I'd seen Wiz act like a real shopkeeper.

It took some doing, but...

"Welcome, welcome, come right in! For a limited time only, all cus-tomers making a purchase of ten thousand eris or more will receive this free Vanir doll that cackles in the night! Spend fifty thousand eris to receive a Vanir mask just like mine! ...Oops! My apologies, boy, but the one I'm wearing is not for sale. Take this specially colored one instead... Come on, now! Welcome, everyone!"

Wiz's eerie employee was proving both an excellent barker and sur-prisingly popular with children.

"Thank you! Thank you very much! Two lighters and a Vanir mask—thank you!"

My Japanese "inventions" were flying off the shelves. Geez. If I'd known business would be this good, I would've started selling them sooner.

"Let me go, Darkness! They stole all my customers, and I'm super upset! Let me show off my art!"

"Aqua, calm down—remember why we're here! Come on, just—take it easy—!"

Darkness physically restrained Aqua from hurting our business any more. Wiz and Vanir, meanwhile, were handling the customers capably.

When the hubbub died down a bit, Vanir came over to us, beaming.

"Fwa-ha-ha-ha-ha-ha! I cannot stop laughing! Look at this! Closing time is still hours away, and we're practically sold out of today's stock of merchandise! I thank you again, boy who thought he was getting somewhere with his friend while they were on vacation but is upset that he's seen no further development since they got home!"

"Wait, are you talking about me?! You are, aren't you?! Wh-wh-whatever! I'm not upset! Megumin, stop shooting me those little glances!"

"I—I am not glancing at anything! Do not let him get to you; demons only say these things to amuse themselves!"

Curse him! He knew exactly what had been on my mind most since getting back from Crimson Magic Village.

"Pair up, make a baby—personally, I couldn't care less. It's just so *depressing* to see you two taking furtive peeks at each other. It would be great if you could find a hotel or a dark alleyway or something and just do it already! But anyway, we have more important things to discuss."

Dammit. I've seriously got to get Aqua over here to take this guy out.

"At this rate, I believe I'll be able to have your three hundred million eris ready by the end of the month. It's not a down payment as such, but let me give you this." Vanir handed me a black mask, the pattern subtly different from that of the one he wore. "A mass-produced Vanir mask, quietly but undeniably popular among the public, one of the true trademark items of this shop. Wear it on the night of a full moon and a mysterious demonic power will raise your magic ability, increase your blood flow, and give your skin a healthy glow—perfect, is it not? And this is an exceptionally rare black variant. You can brag about it to all your little friends."

I...I don't want this.

It won't curse me if I put it on or something, will it...?

5

Ever since that day, Wiz's shop had gotten busier than it had ever been. And today...

"All right, you two. You understand, don't you?"

Yes. It was our long-awaited dinner with the princess.

I was in the living room—Darkness was nowhere to be seen—talking to Aqua and Megumin. Specifically, I was reminding them that we had to avoid embarrassing Darkness.

"Of course I do," Aqua said. "This is a very rare opportunity. I'm going to do the best party trick of my life—all to protect Darkness's good name, naturally. By the way, Kazuma, I was going to do an act where I pull a tiger out of my hat, but there aren't any tigers around here. I thought maybe I'd make do with a Beginner's Bane. That sort of looks like a tiger. Will you help me catch one?"

"I shall surprise and astonish Her Royal Highness with a spectacular entrance such as only the Crimson Magic Clan can perform. I will need something that produces copious amounts of smoke. And fireworks! I will need fireworks. Kazuma, do you know where I might buy such things?"

...I guess Darkness was right to worry.

At the Dustiness mansion.

The biggest house in Axel was on tenterhooks. There normally weren't too many servants there, but today there were lots, maybe to make the place look especially wealthy.

As well it should; Iris, first princess of the nation, had been at the house since the day before.

We were just inside the front door of the mansion. Darkness was there, clad in a simple white dress, her long golden hair tossed over her right shoulder and braided near her neckline. It was just a white dress, but somehow—maybe because she was so attractive to begin with—she made it seem irresistibly sexy. Leading an entourage of servants, she bowed deeply to us and gave an elaborate greeting.

"Honored Kazuma Satou and all our honored guests. I offer you my profound gratitude for taking the time to come to our humble abode today. I, Lalatina Ford Dustiness, shall be your hostess. Please make yourselves at home—all that we have is yours, and we shall expend every effort to ensure your comfort."

No one would have taken her for anything less than a cultured noble's daughter. We acknowledged her hospitality with perfect grace. *Maybe I ought to offer a greeting in return…?*

"We are moist—erm, most honored to be invited here…" I had suddenly stumbled over my words. Darkness, who had been wearing a gentle smile until that moment, turned slightly red and looked at the floor. From the way her shoulders were trembling, I guess she was trying not to laugh. *C-curse her…!*

Dammit. I'm not used to this formal talk. Forget it.

"Hey, Darkness, how about you stop laughing and start hostessing? These clothes are uncomfortable, and it's driving me nuts."

I was wearing a black suit I'd gotten from a rental place. I had tried on a tuxedo and bow tie, but Aqua and Megumin had laughed so hard I swore never to wear it again. The girls' dresses ultimately hadn't been ready in time, and they had been forced to borrow clothes from Darkness.

"If you will please come this way, honored guests."

She ushered us into the house, her shoulders still shaking.

"Kindly wait here a moment. Miss Lalatina is selecting outfits," a servant said, leading us to a sitting room.

After we were seated on a couch, the servant prepared tea and then left us on our own. Soon after, Darkness entered with a different servant and an armful of dresses. She bowed to us, then stood next to the adjoining powder room. She beckoned to Aqua and Megumin. They followed her into the next room, and then…

"Hey, Darkness, the waist is really baggy. I'd like something a little tighter…"

"Th-that's the smallest size I have… Well, don't look at me like that; Crusaders have to have some muscle…! Megumin, what happened to you?"

"It just sort of…drapes. The chest and the hips are too big. Maybe something smaller…"

…I heard the three of them talking.

"I don't have what I don't have… That dress is from when I was a kid. Eeeyow, ow, ow! Megumin, don't pull on my braid!"

The servant joined the conversation, and she must have done some awfully quick tailoring work, because Darkness finally emerged from the powder room with the two girls, looking exhausted.

"…Wow!" I spoke without even realizing it.

Megumin blushed and looked down a little. Her outfit exposed both shoulders, showing plenty of pale skin, which contrasted with the black dress. Unlike her usual jailbait fashion, in this thing she looked downright womanly.

Aqua followed her, wrapped in a white dress.

"Kazuma, look, look! What do you think? The clothes really make the woman, huh?"

I wasn't sure if that was always the case, but the clothes really did suit her in that moment. She had traded her usual blue feather mantle for a snow-white dress. She was so beautiful that I really could have seen someone worshipping her as a goddess—at least, if she could keep her mouth shut.

"Hey, Kazuma," she said, "you've got a whole parade of beautiful women right here in front of you—how about a kind word? A little praise? A touch of worship? I promise the gods won't get mad…"

She really, really needed to keep her mouth shut.

"Yeah, sure, you're all beautiful. Now let's go see the princess. She's been here since yesterday, right?"

Darkness looked profoundly uneasy as I made my primary interest clear. "You swear you won't do anything impolite?" she asked. "You have a tendency to be a little too blunt sometimes. They might overlook a slip or two because adventurers aren't known for their civility—but you understand one wrong word could cost you your head, right?"

Her admonition only made me all the more eager.

A princess. A real live princess. Beautiful, refined royalty who would love flowers and butterflies and little birds.

Then again, apparently she liked adventure stories, so maybe she was more tomboyish than you'd think.

My party and I had failed at everything we'd ever tried, but now we were at a banquet with a member of the royal family coming to see us. I couldn't be blamed for letting it go to my head just a little, could I?

"Okay, you guys, just so you know—I like our house, I really do. We've lived there a long time, and I'm attached to it. But if Her Highness asks me to join her royal guard or something, I'm gonna have to think about it. Just so you're aware."

"Talk about getting ahead of yourself," Darkness said. "We're just having dinner." And then she led us to the main hall.

It was a huge room used to throw feasts. Darkness turned to us again. "All right, are you ready? We're meeting the princess of a whole country, here. Kazuma, in spite of your mouth, I'm convinced you have some good sense, so I'm not too worried about you. But you *did* force me to do chores for you in a maid outfit. If you pull anything here, don't expect to get off scot-free. Aqua, I want you to forget about any flashy party tricks. And *definitely* nothing dangerous. As for you, Megumin... I'm having you searched right now!"

"What?! W-w-w-wait a moment, Darkness—why only me?! And what could you possibly search for? We were just changing together in the same room...! Ahh, hold on! Kazuma is watching! He's staring straight at me!"

As I observed the argument developing in front of me, I asked Aqua, "Just what kind of trick do you plan to do?"

"You make it sound so sordid. This is my big chance to meet the royal family. I'd hate for the princess to be the only one to see my abilities. I thought I'd do a portrait on the spot... A sand picture! Then she can take it home as a memento!"

"Huh. You really do have a lot of talents..."

Meanwhile, right in front of us...

"There, just like I thought! What's this, Megumin? A monster-repellent smoke bomb and a potion that explodes when you open it! What did you think you were going to do with these? I *knew* your chest looked too big..."

"I'm impressed, Darkness, but I have a plan B and a plan C for putting on my performance!"

And so the argument went on. The maid who had been with us ever since getting the dresses ready gave a sigh.

"Whatever she does, I hope I won't get hurt..."

Tell me about it.

6

"Okay, here we go. I'll do most of the talking to Princess Iris, so you guys just stuff your faces and nod along or whatever."

After advising us, Darkness took the lead and opened the door. We found ourselves in a banquet hall. It wasn't showy, but it oozed sophistication. Candles burned inside, giving off quite a bit of light. A number of servants surrounded the table at a distance, waiting silently.

A red carpet had been rolled out, and a rich feast was covering a huge table. At the far end sat a girl in a white dress just like the ones Darkness and Aqua wore. Two other women stood flanking her. One of them was a plain-looking woman in a black dress who carried no weapons. She did, however, have several glittering rings on her fingers, in total defiance of fashion. I guess she was a wizard.

The other attendant was an attractive woman with short hair who wore not a dress but a white suit and carried a sword at her hip.

Presumably, the attendants were women because you might not trust male bodyguards around a girl of that age.

Darkness guided us slowly up to the other three.

"Forgive us for making you wait, Your Highness. These are my friends, adventurers all, Kazuma Satou and his party. Now, you three, the regal individual before you is none other than the first princess of our nation, Princess Iris. Please make your *formal* introductions." She extended a hand and gestured from us to the girl in the middle.

The girl was everything a princess should be and more. She had golden hair, not too long, and clear blue eyes. She was a proper beauty with an air of class, as well as a certain delicacy.

For once, my expectations of this fantasy world hadn't been betrayed. The elf with stick-on ears and his friend, the dwarf with no beard, had been a disappointment; the cat-eared orcs were a nightmare. I had half expected there to be something off about this princess, too.

I was so taken aback, my brain had practically stopped working. Beside me, Aqua gently took the hem of her dress and made a perfect curtsy. Darkness and I both stared in disbelief.

"My name is Aqua, Your Highness, a humble Arch-priest. It is a pleasure to make your acquaintance. Now then, in lieu of a lengthy introduction, I have a trick to show you…"

She tried to go into some sort of routine, but Darkness grabbed her hand.

"I-I'm very sorry, Your Highness, but I must speak with my friend. If you'll excuse us…"

Aqua tugged on Darkness's braid in a show of resistance. While Darkness was distracted, Megumin reached into her skirt and quickly produced a black cape. She must have had it wrapped around her thigh in order to evade Darkness's search.

She opened the cape with a flap and put it over her shoulders, then

flung it back again to begin her dramatic self-introduction. But at that moment, Darkness grabbed her hand, too.

Now our Crusader was grabbing Aqua with one hand and Megumin with the other, while Aqua pulled mercilessly on her braid; Darkness was trying hard to force a smile onto a face that looked ready to dissolve into tears. Aqua showed no sign of letting go of Darkness's hair; she seemed to have taken a liking to the texture.

As I watched, the princess in front of me whispered to the woman in the white suit. Maybe she was too embarrassed to speak aloud.

"Peon, it is not for you to look so openly upon a member of the royal family. You are so far beneath the royal family in stature that you would normally not even be allowed to see its members in person, let alone eat with one of them. Bow your head and do not make eye contact. And more importantly, introduce yourself and start telling stories... So sayeth Her Highness."

I froze in place. A moment later, I understood. Take the samurai era in Japan: Due to differences in social standing, a lord and his retainers wouldn't have eaten in the same room, or at least not at the same time. The way White Suit related things to me like an interpreter was probably because the princess was avoiding even talking directly to those below her.

I had gained some understanding of the nobility by interacting with Darkness and her dad, but this was my first taste of what it meant to meet a royal.

Okay, now I get it.

I said just one word:

"Pass..."

"Your Highness, please, wait just a moment! Nerves have made my friends a little excitable! I'll have a word with them and be right back..."

Darkness grabbed my arm and dragged me to the corner.

*　　*　　*

"What in the world am I going to do with you?! What do you mean, 'pass'?! Why do you think I went out of my way to help you even though it was totally embarrassing to me? Things are completely different here!"

Darkness made to strangle me. I fought back by pulling on her braid.

"I'm the one who should be upset! You said we'd be meeting a princess. I was expecting her to be a little more, you know... *I'm absolutely enchanted by the outside world! Oh brave adventurer, please regale me with stories of your exploits!* How are we supposed to have dinner with *that*? Are you just doing this so you can laugh at us?"

"H-hey, stoppit...! Wh-what *is* it with everybody and pulling my hair today?! S-stop already, save it for when we're alone!" Darkness blushed furiously as she babbled.

I pointed toward Her Highness. "Anyway, should we really be leaving that mess unsupervised? She's already trying to do something..."

Over in the direction I'd pointed, Aqua was putting glue on a piece of paper before tossing sand on it. In a moment's time, she had completed a sand portrait of astonishing accuracy. From a distance, it would have been possible to mistake it for a black-and-white photograph.

"Please accept this as a gesture of my affection for the princess," Aqua said. "I've re-created her likeness, right down to the sauce dribbling from the corner of her mouth."

This untoward statement caused the princess to dab hurriedly at her lips.

"Your Highness! I'll box this boor about the ears—just give me one minute!" Darkness held up the hem of her dress with both hands and rushed at Aqua.

Darkness's threat caused the princess to whisper to White Suit.

"Her Highness forgives the offense," the woman said, "on the grounds that it has allowed her to see a most unusual sight: the calm and taciturn Lalatina in agitation. Adventurers can be expected to be somewhat lacking in civility. More importantly, she requests that you begin telling stories."

As the interpreter spoke, Darkness tried desperately to get the picture from Aqua, who had stuffed it down her dress in an attempt to keep it safe. The princess smiled a little, as if she was amused.

Darkness bowed deeply to her. "My sincere apologies, Your Highness! All I can say is that these three are especially problematic, even among adventurers…!"

Even as she spoke, Aqua whispered, "Here you go!" and passed the picture to the princess.

The girl looked at it and, with an expression of amazement, whispered to White Suit.

"Her Highness says, 'To make such a fine sand picture in such a brief time…! It's wonderful, most excellent!' She offers you a reward."

As she spoke, White Suit took something out of her pocket and gave it to Aqua. It was a small gemstone. I didn't know much about jewels, but even I could tell it must be fairly valuable. Aqua held the pretty stone between her thumb and forefinger, happily watching the light filter through it.

Looking at the ground and red with embarrassment, Darkness seated herself to the right of the princess. Next to Darkness came Megumin, and then Aqua. Her Highness gestured for me to sit on her left.

Shooting little glances at me where I sat politely beside her, the princess whispered to White Suit.

"Her Highness says, 'Are you the one Mitsurugi, gallant bearer of the magic sword, spoke of? Tell us your story.' Personally, I wish to hear it as well. I'm most curious about the man Mitsurugi acknowledges as his superior."

I guess Mitsurugi was pretty well-known among the upper crust of this country. I did wonder, though, exactly what he'd said about me. With White Suit and the princess watching me expectantly, I took a little trip down memory lane…

7

"I saw my chance to set a trap. I deliberately broke the seal, and then left Sylvia stuck inside! And that was how I bought the Crimson Magic Clan enough time to regroup!"

"'Wonderful! So many adventurers have told me their stories, but I've never met people who fight like you do, and I've never heard stories that make my heart race so! Everyone else tells me about how they easily wiped out a whole pack of monsters or bested a dragon in the wilderness with nothing but a sword… They're certainly amazing stories, but they're all about some heroic adventurer who single-handedly defeated a monster…' So Her Highness says."

The princess was listening to my stories of our adventures, her eyes shining like a little girl's. Someone really important was hanging on my every word—could you blame me if I got a little full of myself?

"…Just listen to him," I heard Aqua muttering from across the table.

I ignored her and went on. "That, Princess, is because other adventurers only pick on monsters their own size. That's not necessarily a bad thing, but I for one am always looking to challenge stronger opponents, improving myself every day!"

"'That's wonderful! Would you describe the daily life you lead in your constant pursuit of self-improvement?' …So asks Her Highness. I'm rather curious myself…"

The princess and White Suit seemed genuinely impressed.

"Well, let's see… I'm careful never to leave the house during the day, so as to store up my energy; I only go out come nighttime. I make a quiet patrol of the town, trying to do my part to preserve public safety."

I had barely touched the lavish feast that lay before me. I only took a sip of my drink every now and then as I spoke.

On the far side of the table, Megumin had started to whisper, too. "Aqua, that man just lolls around all day long, then goes out and wanders the streets at night. And he dares to pass off that dissolute life-style as keeping the peace?"

"Shh, I want to see where this goes. You know this guy; he'll get carried away for sure. Give him enough rope and he'll hang himself, just you watch…"

Not likely. I wasn't *that* stupid.

I chose my words carefully, keeping a close eye on the princess's reaction. When I glanced at Darkness, I found she was looking at the ground as if she was embarrassed. Megumin, in the seat next to hers, was fiddling with Darkness's braid. It looked like she'd taken a liking to the feel of it, too. Darkness, having realized that the girls seemed to behave themselves as long as they were playing with her hair, was letting Megumin do as she pleased.

The princess gave a contented sigh and whispered to White Suit.

"'You're a most unusual adventurer, aren't you? You're different, somehow, from the others I've met. What did you do before you entered adventuring?' …Her Highness wants to know."

Employment history, huh? I thought fondly back on my life in Japan.

"Before I came to this country, I worked to ensure my family would always have a place to come home to. Day after day, I silently polished my skills, protecting that most precious of places from encroaching catastrophe. But it was sad work, for no one understood or valued what I did…"

That prompted White Suit to say, "Hmm. Something like a soldier protecting the castle in the capital, then? They, too, often go overlooked. Although perhaps that's a sign of just how safe the capital is… So you also kept your homeland safe from disaster, an unsung hero."

I gave a deep nod. "My tasks were many. I asked little more than a contract of three months or so, and I repelled those who sought to steal my employer's goods."

You guessed it. I was a paperboy and a part-time collector of electric bills.

White Suit looked at me in amazement, and this time she was the one who turned to whisper to the princess. I caught snatches of their conversation: "To seek a contract... Surely fought off demons... Employer's goods... Done battle with thieves..."

Aqua was focused on me as if she wanted to say something. I quickly looked away, but I could feel her eyes on me.

Stop! It's all true, more or less. Don't look at me like that...

8

It happened around the time we were all well fed and the talk was flowing smoothly. I had gone right on chatting away when White Suit suddenly said, "I can't believe you really beat the hero Mitsurugi, with his magic sword... Pardon me for being terribly rude, but could I see your Adventurer's Card, Mr. Kazuma? I think I might learn something from how you've distributed your skill points..."

Gosh. What a thing to ask. No way could I show her my weird-ass Adventurer's Card. If she wanted to know where I'd learned Lich skills, I'd be in real trouble. Megumin, sensing that I was starting to panic, said, "Ahem, we adventurers do have our trade secrets. I know you're one of Her Highness's attendants, but even so... Oh! It's been such a lovely meal—Aqua, maybe you'd like to show off your most legendary trick..."

She took the bullet for me, doing everything she could to change the subject. And here came Aqua to help...!

"...? I drew a great sand picture today, and now I'm all done. Gee, Megumin, were you that eager to see my tricks? Well, all right, if I feel like it, I'll show you something absolutely incredible tomorrow. Hey, bring me more of this wine—more wine!"

Aqua was in fine oblivious form, as always, as she demanded a refill from one of the servants. White Suit gave me a dubious look.

"We're part of the nobility, not fellow adventurers. We won't share Mr. Kazuma's information with anyone else. But a study of his skills may help us strengthen the Royal Army. All people long to defeat the Demon King. Won't you help us come one step closer to realizing this goal? Or is there some reason you can't show us your card?"

Yes. Yes, there is.

Then Darkness spoke up, looking at White Suit with a gentle smile. "This man is an Adventurer, said to be the weakest class. No doubt he was embarrassed for you to find out. Perhaps you could allow me to examine his card in your stead?"

"Y-yeah, that's right. Somehow I never quite got around to mentioning it, but I'm of the weakest class. Gee, what a… What a shame you found out," I said, scratching my head in embarrassment.

At this, White Suit's attitude changed to one of exasperation. "Really, an Adventurer? I'm starting to wonder if you did everything you've been claiming. You say you defeated Mitsurugi in a fight, but is it true? If it is, why don't you explain to us how exactly you beat him?"

Her tone was polite, but it was obvious she had her suspicions about me. I figured it would look bad if I admitted I'd defeated Mitsurugi by ambushing him with Steal.

But then, the princess tugged on White Suit's sleeve. She whispered in the woman's ear, looking at me. White Suit seemed a bit confused, but after a moment, she came out with it.

"…Ah, ahem… 'I can't believe someone of the weakest class could best someone as handsome as Mitsurugi. Surely you aren't lying to me, a member of the royal family? His fame as a Sword Master and bearer of a magic blade is known throughout the capital. I seriously doubt a novice of the weakest class defeated him. Especially with his being so handsome.' So… So says Her Highness. And I concur. He is quite handsome."

"All right, listen, I'm a pretty laid-back guy, but if you keep flapping your gums, I'm gonna give you a spanking." I was getting pretty fed up with all the talk of "handsome" this and "handsome" that, especially seeing as it wasn't a word that was being used to describe me, and I lost my head a little. Yes: I acted just like I always do, completely forgetting I was dealing with royalty.

This immediately made White Suit very upset.

"You lout! How dare you speak that way to Her Highness!" Even as she shouted, her sword was already in her hands.

Oh, crap!

"My humblest apologies for my companion's impetuousness! This man has no sense of civility whatsoever, so please, for my sake, have mercy on him! His proud record in battle is the truth—isn't that what Princess Iris came to hear about? To then punish him for it—well, think of your reputation...!" Darkness was furiously bowing her head.

At that, the princess whispered to White Suit.

"Princess Iris proclaims that in deference to the Dustiness family, which has served our kingdom so long and so faithfully, she will let this affront go unpunished. But her mood has been soured. She will offer a proper reward for these adventure stories. The weakling-class liar is advised to take it and go."

Geez, that hurts!

Darkness had really saved my skin. But the way they'd spoken to me had just begged for a comeback—how dare they get so angry when I obliged? I was just about to up and leave when...

"Eeeyow, ow, ow! Hey, Megumin, what are you—?!"

The shout came from Darkness. Apparently, our wizard had gone from playing with Darkness's braid to giving it an angry pull. I found myself going as pale as Darkness. Megumin probably valued her companions more than anyone else in our party.

When everyone else had been running from Sylvia in Crimson Magic Village, and Megumin heard that fleeing would mean only more trouble for us later, she was the one who faced our opponent—a general of the Demon King—head-on. She had a tradition of never refusing a fight and was by far the most short-tempered and least patient of all of us. Given the situation, I was certain trouble was brewing.

"…"

Megumin was silent at first, adding several additional violent tugs on Darkness's braid. As if that was all it took to make her feel better, she then let go of Darkness's hair and returned to the business of eating.

Geez, and here I was terrified she was about to be all, *Just you say that again!* or something. Talk about anticlimactic.

While the princess and White Suit still stood in shock, Darkness, sounding mystified, said, "…Megumin, you've been awfully well behaved today. I was sure you were about to blow something up…"

Megumin silently brought some food to her mouth, chewed it, and swallowed. Only then did she say quietly, "If I were by myself, I would certainly not hold back. But if I caused trouble here, it would only make more problems for you, Darkness."

And then she resumed eating. We stared at her.

Darkness was silent for a moment. Then she stood in place and bowed to the princess. "My apologies, Your Highness, but I humbly ask you to take back what you said about this man being a liar. Exaggerate he surely does, but nothing he's said is untrue. And he may be the weakest class, but when you really need him, he can be counted on more than anyone I know. I implore you, Princess, reconsider what you've said and apologize to him."

White Suit stiffened at this. "Miss Dustiness, are you suggesting Princess Iris would apologize to a mere commoner?"

This time it was the princess who stood. Then she spoke, loudly enough that even I could hear her.

"I will not apologize. If you say he is no liar, then have him tell me how he defeated Mitsurugi. If he can't, then he's nothing but a weak, foul—?!"

She was cut off in the middle of her tirade by a slap from Darkness.

"*What* are you doing, Miss Dustiness?!" White Suit stood openmouthed before flinging herself at Darkness in a white-hot rage.

"Oh! D-don't…!" Iris stuttered, but she was too quiet for White Suit to hear. The woman's sword came down at Darkness…

"?!"

...and, to our collective horror, bit into her pale arm with a dull sound. Bright-red blood erupted from it, covering Darkness and the princess, along with White Suit.

White Suit didn't move—or rather, couldn't. She had probably meant to cut Darkness's arm clean off, but instead the blow had only nicked the skin and muscle.

Not sparing a glance for White Suit, who looked on in astonishment, Darkness silently turned to the princess.

That was our Crusader, and boy, was she tough. Maybe the toughest in the whole kingdom.

"I apologize for my rudeness, Your Highness. But this man has fought well and done many great deeds, and I am not simply covering for him. He has no obligation to explain his victory over Mitsurugi, nor do you have any right to deride him if he doesn't."

Darkness spoke quietly, patting the princess's reddened cheek, almost as though she were gently lecturing a child—with her arm bleeding the whole time.

Iris looked at her in total shock. I stood and spoke to White Suit, who was still looking on in pale-faced amazement.

"...Okay, fine. My friends have worked so hard to stick up for me, I guess I should come clean. I'll *show* you how I defeated Mitsurugi. But it's not very cool, okay?"

The woman's eyes went even bigger at that, but she resumed her fighting stance, sword in hand.

"That's enough! Enough, Claire! Stop this!" The princess's voice was almost a scream. The overwhelming sense of tension I had felt from her just moments before was gone. What had caused her to change so quickly? Maybe she was just a spoiled little girl?

"...If you want to, I won't stop you. Do it, Kazuma. It's not like you're gonna lose, right?" Darkness laughed, egging me on, even as she pressed one hand to her wound.

I leaped at White Suit. "Damn straight! Think of everyone I've

fought! Magic sword guys and Demon King's generals and bounty hunt-
ers! They're my bread and butter! You know what comes next—*Steal*!!"

White Suit obviously had no idea what was coming. I would steal
her sword, and then…!

…I would stand here awkwardly, apparently.

Instead, I apologized to her in a small voice. "Sorry. I'll… I'll give
these back…"

"Huh? You'll— Oh… Ahhhhh!"

The white-suited woman dropped her sword as she desperately
checked her lower body. I held out a pair of white panties, embarrassed.

"You impossible, impossible man! Why can't you ever just be cool
for a change?!"

9

"I'm…sorry about what happened…"

White Suit was apologizing to us. Beside her, the princess had buried her face in White Suit's arm as if she was trying to hide.

"Pay it no mind," Darkness said. "We were impertinent as well. As
you can see, we were able to heal my wound without so much as a scar. I
think it would be best if we all considered this water under the bridge."
She smiled sweetly as she spoke.

That brought an embarrassed tinge to White Suit's cheeks. Apparently, neither she nor the princess really cared anymore how I had beaten
Mitsurugi.

"…Just the same, to heal an injury like that in the blink of an eye…
You must have a truly gifted Arch-priest," White Suit said, glancing at
Aqua, who was stretched out on the table.

I'd thought Aqua was being awfully quiet, but really she had gotten drunk all by herself and was sleeping it off. We'd had to smack her
awake to cure Darkness, but the moment she'd done so, she blacked out
again. *Oh well. If she were awake, she'd just say something obnoxious. Let
sleeping goddesses lie, I guess.*

White Suit continued. "And Lady Dustiness, that toughness! And from the color of her eyes, I'm guessing your friend there is of the Crimson Magic Clan… With a party like this, I shouldn't be surprised that you've taken out several generals of the Demon King. Although, well, when it comes to Mr. Kazuma…" For some reason, I was the only one she cast a dubious look at. Maybe she still hadn't forgiven me for stealing her panties earlier.

Then the trembling princess whispered. Not to White Suit but to her other attendant, the mage, who I'd almost forgotten about because she hadn't spoken a word or even moved this entire time.

"Your Highness, I think it would be better if you said that yourself. It's all right; I've been watching Mr. Kazuma, and I believe he has a soft spot for people like you."

Wait a second—we just met, and she's already branding me a jailbait enthusiast?

The princess came up to me, not taking her eyes off the ground.

"…I'm sorry I called you a liar. Will you…let me hear about your adventures again?" She was clearly embarrassed, but she managed to look at me while she spoke.

"Gladly!"

"Well, then. We'll be going back to the castle now. Lady Dustiness and everyone, thank you, and we apologize for the trouble," the mage said.

Beside her, the princess wore an enthusiastic smile that looked much more suited to her age than her earlier expressions had.

"No, thank *you*. We're sorry we couldn't be better hosts…" Darkness spoke with a smile on her face. "Your Highness, let's speak again next time we're around the castle. I promise I'll have lots of good adventure stories for you." This made the princess smile even wider.

Somehow, the two of them looked like a pair of sisters, where the older one cared about the younger and the younger admired the older. Watching the pleasant scene, the mage began to chant Teleport.

...Okay, here we go.

"Now, then. You have all achieved a great deal, and your exploits will no doubt go down in the history of our kingdom, to be related to future generations. In recognition of your deeds, we offer you these."

As she spoke, White Suit took out an award certificate and some kind of pouch...

...and gave it, not to me, but to Darkness.

...Well, that's just fine!

"Goodness, thank you very much." Darkness accepted the items with a gracious smile, then said, "All right then, Your Highness. Take care of yourself...!" She and Megumin both waved good-bye.

"Okay, Princess. I'll come by to tell you some more stories someday." And I started waving, too.

The mage had nearly finished her Teleport incantation when the princess took my arm.

"What are you saying?" she asked with a look of confusion.

"Teleport!"

I closed my eyes. Light engulfed both the princess and me.

When I could bring myself to look again, I found the girl smiling innocently, a huge castle behind her. Apparently, I'd been teleported right along with her.

""Your Highness?!"" White Suit and the mage exclaimed together.

"You said you'd come by to tell me some more stories, didn't you?" the princess said, and then she smiled at me.

I guess that's royalty for you. They always get what they want.

Chapter 2

May I Reeducate This Intelligent Girl!

1

The world was shrouded in darkness; it wouldn't be unusual for most people to be in bed around this time.

But despite the hour...

""""Welcome back, Your Highness!""""

A host of servants offered a greeting almost as though they'd been waiting for us.

We were in the great hall of the castle in the center of the country's capital. I could barely process any of it for wondering how I'd gotten myself into this. I could only follow the princess's lead.

She and White Suit showed me to a luxurious room on one of the castle's upper floors. Then White Suit said she had to make a report and disappeared somewhere, leaving the princess and the mage woman and me.

The people we had passed on the way didn't give me any perturbed looks; they just offered a slight bow and went about their business. *Not to be too self-deprecating, but are they sure they want to leave someone like me alone to wander the castle freely?*

What to do, what to do? I really wanted to go home. Never mind the fact that until just a little while ago, I'd been so taken with the princess that if she had asked me to be her personal knight, I would have seriously considered it.

As I stood there, still panicked over my sudden kidnapping, Iris whispered to her mage. The woman nodded and then said to me with a smile:

"'Mr. Kazuma Satou, welcome to our castle. As you've been invited here as a guest, there's no need to stand on ceremony or take undue consideration. Please make yourself at home. For the time being, this room shall be yours. Now, then. More adventure stories!' ...So sayeth the princess."

"I'm sorry, Miss, uh...Miss Mage. Could you, um, come here for just a second?" I retreated to one corner of the room and gestured to the mage.

"Yes? Oh, you can call me Lain. There's no need to be particularly formal with me. I'm a noble after a fashion but from a very small house, not worth comparing with the Dustiness family. As a friend of Lady Dustiness, you practically rank higher than me."

"Okay, then. Miss Lain. Can I ask you something?"

"No need to be formal. You don't have to afford me any special form of address at all... Anyway, yes, what is it?"

She sounded a bit disappointed, but she was an older, noble mage, and a woman to boot. I didn't have the nerve to call her by her name alone when we'd only just been introduced. Especially not after White Suit had spent the entire time at Darkness's house berating me for being rude. And now I didn't have Darkness to cover for me in the event of any faux pas. Even if Lain said it was all right, I couldn't help hedging my bets.

With one eye on the princess, who looked a little bored, I said quietly, "So, uh, Miss Lain. I'd like to get an explanation somewhere along the line here. I know the princess said she invited me as a guest, but... this is really a kidnapping, isn't it?"

"No, you've really been invited as a guest. Not kidnapped."

"I've totally been kidnapped!"

Lain ignored my interjection but leaned a little closer and whispered:

"…I can tell you, I've never seen the princess act this way in her entire life. She's normally an upstanding member of the royal family and doesn't cause trouble for anyone. And there's no one in this castle who's of both the right age and the right social status to play with her. Please indulge this first act of selfishness and stay to be her playmate for a while. Won't you?"

……*Ummm…*

"That's not really the point. To be completely honest, I pretty much told her all my adventure stories earlier. Maybe you could be so kind as to tell her that so she'll let me go home? Just say I'm fresh out of stories."

So Lain went back over to the princess and whispered all this to her. Eventually…

"She says…'I brought you here as a little bit of payback to Lalatina for slapping me.'" Beside the mage, Iris was listening to this with a certain despondence. "'And also because you and Lalatina and your friends looked like you were having a lot of fun, and I was jealous… I'm sorry for suddenly doing something so selfish. Please, will you play with me? Even for just a few days?'"

…Okay, that's pretty sweet. Really, all they're asking is for me to be the princess's playmate for a while, right? And if I say no, she'll just get upset, and then Darkness's reputation will be down the drain, right? Can't let that happen.

"…All right. Okay, then, why don't I tell you a little bit about Darkness…I mean, Lalatina? Miss Lain, if you could be so kind as to explain to my friends that I'm staying here for a little bit? I wouldn't want them to worry."

She agreed to my request and left. Suddenly, the princess and I were alone in the opulent room.

Well, sort of. Two female knights stood just outside the door, probably the princess's bodyguards. But still, a lot of unsettling questions ran through my mind: Did they really want to leave a girl of her age alone at night with a young man? Especially some weirdo they'd just met and dragged here? Even if I explained this was all the princess's doing, I couldn't imagine the king or the other VIPs taking this lightly if they found out.

The princess seemed to read my thoughts. She smiled and said, "My father is with my older brother and the generals, heading for the town where they're going to make their stand against the Demon King. And nobody will get upset about a little thing like this… When it's just the two of us, you can talk to me just like you do to Lalatina—or Darkness, I guess you call her. Please, tell me everything about life outside the castle."

She sat on the bed, eager to listen.

2

White Suit came back after she had finished delivering her reports and taking care of procedures.

"Pardon me. Your Highness, I've made the arrangements. Mr. Kazuma, you're our official guest now, so please, be at liberty here in the castle."

I was right at the climax of the story I was telling.

"And then Darkness says, 'Erg… H-how did this happen…?' And then, naked as the day she was born, she goes around behind me, red up to her ears, takes my towel, and filled with shame, she…"

"And? And what?!"

"*And what*, indeed! Teaching Princess Iris things like that—do you *want* me to cut you down?!"

White Suit took in the sight of the princess, lying on the bed listening to me with rapt attention, and jumped between us as if to cover her. Her sword was out of its scabbard as she shouted at me.

"H-hang on a second! Just a minute! Iris said she really wanted to hear—"

"How dare you! You, a lowly adventurer, presume to refer to Her

Highness without so much as a title of respect? You will call her 'Your Highness'! And you will speak to her with proper formality!"

G-geez, this lady's a pain!

"Stand down, Claire. I told Master Kazuma that he could call me by my name, and further that he should speak naturally to me. B-but anyway. Master Kazuma, what did... What did Lalatina do, naked and embarrassed and with your towel? You must tell me!"

"No, Your Highness! You mustn't listen to such stories, and Master Kazuma, you mustn't tell them to her! A-anyway, surely the rumors that you and Lady Dustiness were in the bath together are—are only rumors, aren't they?"

The princess had been lying on the bed, her fists clenched in eager anticipation of the outcome of my tale. She urged me to continue. I sat on a chair and spoke to White Suit, aka Claire, who seemed every bit as intent on hearing my story as Her Highness was.

"I haven't said a single untrue thing. If you don't believe me—well, a castle this big must have one of those, you know, those bells like they use in big-city police stations during interrogations to find out if you're telling the truth. The ones that ring when you tell a lie? You could bring in one of those if you want."

That seemed to convince her I was telling the truth. For the moment, Claire put her sword away, but she glared at me and said, "Let's say I believe you. I admit I've done nothing but doubt you since our meeting at Lady Dustiness's manor. But all the same, I must ask you not to tell Princess Iris such stories!"

"I'm of the impression that the decision of whether or not to listen to my stories is Princess Iris's to make. Surely Her Highness's handmaiden is not the one to mete out orders. Consider her royal disappointment at being interrupted just when she was listening with such interest! Go on, scat! I'm gonna finish my story, so beat it!"

"You think I'd let you finish a story like that? And I am no mere handmaiden! I am Claire, eldest daughter of the Sinfonia family, a house no less noble than that of the Dustinesses, who seem to be so fond of you. I am Princess Iris's bodyguard, and…"

She started babbling on about her accomplishments. I ignored her, instead saying to Iris, "Well, if White Suit here says that story is off-limits, how about a different one?"

"Wh-White Suit! You barbarian, you shall refer to me as Lady Claire! Argh, I am so sick of you! I can't imagine how much Lady Dustiness must suffer every day…"

Claire's aggressive attitude must have registered with the princess, because with evident disappointment, she said, "I guess we don't have a choice… It's a shame, but we'll have to postpone the rest until another time."

This obedient declaration earned a sigh of relief from Claire. *I see—I guess Iris really is a good little girl most of the time.*

"All right, something else, then. Once Darkness and I had a duel, and whoever lost would have something awful done to them. So let me tell you what happened when I won…"

"Y-y-yes, absolutely! I want to hear that one!"

"A-absolutely not! Your Highness, you must not listen to this man! He is a bad, bad man!"

3

It must have been past midnight. Claire had been listening to my stories along with the princess, blowing up at me, then blowing up at me again, and finally, for a change, blowing up at me. It kept her very busy.

But all that rage must have finally tired her out, because she had collapsed on the bed where the princess sat and fallen asleep.

As for the princess, my stories must have really struck a chord with her, because she was still listening intently, showing no signs of getting sleepy. We had really hit it off, and formalities were out the window. However, I had long ago run out of both my own stories and those about my friends.

"Really? Tell me more about this 'culture festival' at this 'school' of yours!"

"More? Well, it's just for kids about your age, Iris, and they do all these presentations. Like, some of them might set up a pretend café."

Our conversation had turned to the country I'd come from. I just told her it was somewhere very far away, omitting the fact that it was also in another world. The princess seemed awfully jealous just hearing about my life at school; she had never even seen Japan, but she already looked like someone thinking fondly of home.

There were no monsters; kids her age got to study and play in peace every day. It was a life that had seemed totally boring to me, but for her...

"Your country sounds like so much fun! It's like something out of a dream. I can't believe it... But trying to run a pretend café with people my age? What do they do when some derelict comes in and says he won't pay? And isn't that an awful lot of people working one location? Do they really make enough profit to cover everyone's salary?"

She seemed to think I'd had a life worth envying.

I smiled at the princess—she was so much younger than me. "The point of the 'café' is to have fun. They're not really out to make money. It's...almost like playing make-believe. Everyone wears their school uniforms and tries to attract customers. It's all in good fun."

The princess looked more envious than ever—but also just a little sad. And I guess that made sense.

This girl was royalty. She had no commoner friends, and she'd never been to school.

In this world, it seemed like no one except the highly intelligent Crimson Magic Clan, with their unique culture, had compulsory education. It wasn't on a big scale, but the clan did make sure everybody attended school from the time they were small. From that perspective, maybe they really were ahead of the curve.

...Even if they were also completely insane.

"School...," the princess whispered, longing in her voice.

I said casually to her, "If you like the idea that much, how about you start a school here? I'll bet it couldn't hurt. And it would definitely help the nation as a whole."

Just for a second, the princess looked like she was going to say something, but then she stopped.

…?

As I was wondering what was going on, a clanging bell shattered the night's quiet. It caused Claire to spring up from where she was sleeping. She collected herself quickly despite the rude awakening.

"…Ugh, again?" she muttered, then jumped off the bed and rushed out of the room.

What? What again?

Before I could ask, a voice boomed through the town. It sounded like the emergency quest announcements we occasionally got in Axel.

"Demon King army attack warning! Demon King army attack warning! All knights, sortie immediately. All adventurers are to help preserve public order. Come to the center of town and prepare to repel any monster attack. All high-level adventurers, we request your cooperation!"

The announcement had brought a sad smile to the princess's face.

"You see how it is. We don't have the leisure to focus on schooling," she murmured.

Then I remembered something Aqua had said to me before we came to this world.

She'd told me things were tough here because of some guy called the Demon King.

4

"The night attack by the Demon King has been repelled. We thank all adventurers for their cooperation. Compensation will be offered to all those who participated in the battle. Please stop by the desk at the Adventurer's Guild to claim your reward."

The announcement came less than an hour after Claire had run out of the room. They'd dealt with things surprisingly quickly. But this was supposed to be the capital of this country. If the Demon King could just launch a night attack any old time he wanted—didn't that speak to a pretty dire tactical situation?

What were all the reincarnated cheaters from Japan doing? They needed to step it up!

I guess they probably wouldn't want to hear that from me, given how little help I would be to them. Sheesh! I'd love to just leave the front lines behind me...

Maybe the look on my face gave me away.

"...Thank you for such a pleasant chat. Once the sun rises, you can have Lain take you back to your town. Would you apologize to Lalatina for me? I did take you away without asking... We're not exactly on the front lines of the war with the Demon King, but attacks like this do occur from time to time. It's not entirely safe."

It almost sounded like the princess was concerned for me.

Even if I stuck around, I couldn't protect this city. I couldn't even help. I felt bad for the princess, but it would be best for me to get out of the line of fire as quickly as I could.

"Thank you for going along with my bout of selfishness today, Master Kazuma," Iris said. "Perhaps you could...tell me more adventure stories some other time?" She gave me a girlish smile.

Damn, she's pretty cute.

She spent all her time surrounded by servants and officials, never having any friends her own age to play with. *I guess a story now and again wouldn't hurt...*

Her lovely, innocent face left me feeling a bit awkward. I smiled back at her, trying to hide it.

"Well, sure. To be honest, I'm pretty much a coward, so I'd like to go home as soon as I can. But for you? I'll make sure to do lots of interesting things, and then I'll come tell you about them."

She looked at me, genuinely thrilled. "Hee-hee! Thank you.

Somehow…you…remind me of how my older brother used to be. I do have an older brother, you know, but in a royal family, even close relatives turn formal after a certain point. He and I don't talk like this anymore… The truth is, I wish you could stay a little longer, but it wouldn't be fair to ask any more of you…"

"I'm sorry, what did you say?" She'd said it so casually.

With some embarrassment, she answered, "…Huh? Er, um…I…I really wish you could stay a little longer…"

But that wasn't what I'd been asking about.

"I…I said this is how it used to be with my older brother…"

"That. Kindly say that again, please."

"Y-you remind me of my elder brother," she said hesitantly.

"Not so formally, if you don't mind."

Then she said it.

"You're like my big brother…"

I decided to stay at the castle.

5

Tok, tok.

A knock came at my door, a thoughtful knock that wasn't so loud as to upset the person in the room. I opened my eyes at the sound, confused to find myself in a strange place.

"Master Kazuma, are you awake? I've brought your breakfast." The voice on the other side of the door jogged my memory of the events of the previous night.

That's right. I had decided to live in this castle, starting today.

"Good morning. I'm up."

That brought an acknowledgment from the other side of the door, and then a white-haired old man in a tuxedo appeared. I sat up in bed, and the old probably-a-butler wheeled in a cart loaded with food.

Let's call him Sebastian.

"For breakfast today, we have Lesser Dragon bacon and fried eggs and a vegetable salad with plenty of fresh asparagus. Please choose any bread you like to go with it. The vegetables for the salad were picked just this morning. Asparagus has a high Attack value, so please take care that it doesn't bite back."

The old man set the food by the side of my bed while running down a menu that offered any number of chances for a smart remark. It was shocking enough to think that a dragon, the king of any fantasy world, might show up in bacon form, but powerful, aggressive asparagus was unsettling, too.

Maybe I should start with the easiest food. That would be the eggs.

And so, with impeccably poor grace, I leaned over in bed and speared the fried eggs with my fork.

"Kyuu!"

...Kyuu?

I froze when the eggs gave a cry. Slowly, I looked down at my plate, but at that moment, another knock came at the door.

"Come in," I said, giving up on the eggs. The door opened gently.

"G-good morning..."

There, half-hidden in the shadow of the door, stood Iris, speaking softly and acting a little embarrassed. She looked over at me but hesitated to come in.

Well, this is a new side of her. I wonder what's going on.

The women in my circle surely would have stood in front of the door crying, kicked it down, or threatened to blow it up with magic if I didn't come out.

"Good... Good morning, Your Highness. We were talking until quite late last night—I'm surprised to see you up so early."

"Um, so long as we're in the castle, I'd be happy if you wouldn't be so formal with me, if possible..."

We exchanged these hesitant greetings, then looked at each other awkwardly. I *had* been less formal yesterday, but that was in the middle of the night, and there had been kind of a weird tension between us.

Iris seemed to be a little calmer, too, now that it was morning. She was shooting me little glances, looking a bit embarrassed.

"You think? Okay, let's go again."

"Right! G-good morning, Big, um, Big Brother…!"

Big Brother! Those words made the tension rise in spite of the early hour, but if I made a stir about it, I would frighten Iris. Minding my gentlemanly manners, I got out of bed and gave her an indulgent smile. Maybe my mature behavior made her feel shy, because she went just a little bit red. It was adorable.

"Morning, Iris."

"…Um, thank you, but…please put on some pants…"

Once I was fully dressed and had eaten, I went on a walk through the castle with Iris.

"You've got it all wrong, Iris—I swear I'm not some kind of weirdo. I just didn't have any pajamas, so I was sleeping in my underwear this one night…"

"I understand! I know that now, so could you please stop talking about it, Elder Brother?"

Iris hadn't called me Big Brother since the events of that morning. It was Elder Brother now, a term with a definite sense of distance.

When I asked what I should be doing in the castle, I was given to understand that I should just talk about things that Iris didn't know or that might catch her interest.

"So I should kind of think of myself as your teacher, then."

"No, you shouldn't. Claire and Lain are my teachers. You're more of—maybe a playmate?"

Beside me, Iris's apologetic voice grew smaller and smaller, and finally she looked at the ground.

This girl was the most important person in the castle at the moment, so I wished she would be a little clearer on what she wanted. Maybe I could do something about this shyness. Iris had finished higher education, which made her strangely adult—maybe she was trying to be considerate toward those around her. She well understood how much power the royal family held and how much consternation she could cause for those around her with just a single self-indulgent demand.

Lain, the mage, had said that dragging me to this castle was the first selfish thing the princess had ever done. Apparently, she'd done it partly as a way to get back at Darkness, but at the same time, if all I had to do was be the royal playmate in order to earn a rich life in the castle, well, that didn't sound so bad.

Lost in conversation, Iris and I found ourselves at the castle gardens. There were some parasols set up there, along with chairs and a table with a board game on it.

"Actually, I don't have any lessons today, so I thought perhaps we could play this game together…" Her invitation was hesitant, as if she was afraid I might refuse.

I sat down and started lining pieces up on the board. "I'm not one of your servants, Iris, so don't expect me to let you win after putting up a little fight. When I play, I play for real. They haven't yet made a game I've lost at. You sure you wanna do this?"

"! Y-yes! That's just what I want! Nobody in the castle will ever play against me—maybe they think they're being polite. But I don't mind losing! I really don't, so please, give it everything you've got!"

"I like your spirit! Now, you won't cry when I beat you, right? If you do, I bet I'll get in a lot of trouble. Okay, here we go! If we're really being serious, then we should start by wishing our opponent luck. Good luck!"

"Good luck!"

Then I made my first move…!

"Uh… Um, it's getting dark out. Do you think maybe we could stop for today?"

"As if! Think you're gonna win and then just ditch me? I told you, when I play, I play for real! I finally know all your little quirks, so now it's just a matter of time till I beat you. Oh, and incidentally, don't hold back just 'cause you want to wrap up, okay? If you let me win, I'll know!"

"I know I was the one who wanted to play in the first place, but you can be an awfully annoying person, Elder Brother!"

"Whatever! I hate this stupid game anyway! One of my party members loves this game, but every time I get teleported, it drives me nuts!"

"Well, saying that to me doesn't help much, does it?"

As we sat there arguing over the game board, Claire came running up to us, her face pale.

"I come back from getting dinner ready, and what do I find?! How dare you speak to the princess that way! Acknowledge your defeat like a man and come eat dinner before it gets cold! It isn't your place to cause trouble for Princess Iris!"

"Damn it all! Thanks a lot, Claire. We'll finish this tomorrow! And I'll win for sure!"

"You child! You're being such a child, Elder Brother!"

"Elder Brother?! Y-Your Highness, do you mean *him*?!"

Only the heated argument between Claire and me disturbed the tranquil, aristocratic atmosphere of the castle.

And that was how I became the princess's playmate.

6

I could hear Lain talking in the room.

"—and so for that reason, members of the royal line have been born with more pronounced talents than the common people. Taking the hero who defeats the Demon King as a husband is more than simply a reward for that hero."

Apparently, they were in the middle of history class. But it didn't matter to me; I knocked on the door anyway.

"...Master Kazuma. I'm very sorry, but Princess Iris is studying right now. Perhaps I could ask you to come back later." Lain, the instructor, spoke without letting much emotion show on her face.

"How much later is later? Five minutes?"

"Erm, no. Today, Her Highness will be busy with history class until evening."

I peeked into the room. Iris looked at me and fidgeted. I guess no one had ever invited her to come play before, and she was happy about it. But she couldn't really say that she wanted to quit class and go have fun, so there was a bit of trepidation mingled with her happiness.

"Sure, okay, fine. I'll be killing time outside, then."

"Thank you, please do. If you'll excuse us, then…," Lain said with a relieved sigh.

I left the room. Iris looked a bit disappointed, but there were some things even I didn't have a choice in. I went into the garden and set up shop right outside the room where Iris was having class…

"I wiiish I could flyyy in the skyyy like my bamboo dragonflyyyy!"

I took out the bamboo dragonfly, a product I'd developed that Vanir had nixed, and began singing an advertising ditty at the top of my lungs. I was just sending it up into the air when the window flew open.

"Master Kazuma! Princess Iris is finding it most difficult to concentrate on her studies, so perhaps you could find somewhere else to sing and play!"

I passed the time trying my best to make study impossible. Finally Iris rushed out, class apparently over.

"Elder Brother, what was that magical device you had?! It looked like so much fun! Let me…try it…too…"

She really had come running; she was out of breath.

"Oh, you mean this? It's a state-of-the-art magical device imbued with wind magic. It has unlimited uses. Just spin it around like this, and you can make it fly as many times as you want."

"Wow! A magical device with unlimited uses is practically a divine item!"

She was so quick to believe what I'd told her. I gave her the bamboo dragonfly.

"How about we play a game? If you can meet a certain condition, I might give this to you as a present..."

"R-really?! Tell me, tell me! What condition?"

Ten minutes later...

"There! Checkmate! I wiiiin!"

"Uh-huh, you sure do. I lose. Gosh, Elder Brother, you really are like a child."

"What's this? Such arrogance, even in defeat. Well anyway, here's the dragonfly, just like I promised."

"Th-thank you! But...can I really have it? All I did was play a game at a one-piece handicap, and this is a powerful magical item..." Iris held the bamboo dragonfly carefully in both hands and spoke to me apologetically.

At that moment, someone called out to us.

"So this is where you've been, Your Highness. You went running off and left me, your poor bodyguard, and I've been looking for you ever since... Ah, Master Kazuma. Is that a bamboo dragonfly you have? I met an adventurer with a rather odd name once who made me something similar."

Apparently, Lain had been looking all over for Iris, who had dashed for freedom as soon as class was over.

"You know who made this magical item, Lain? It's wonderful, practically divine...!"

"Magical item? No, that's... It's just made of cut bamboo. It's a children's toy—anyone who knows how can make—"

Before Lain could finish, Iris's eyes welled up with tears and she glared at me. "Elder Brother, you liar! This won't stand—that win of yours doesn't count!"

"Hey now, what did I say yesterday? I said I was playing as hard as I could and still couldn't beat you. And I also said that if you can't win on skill, you have to find some other advantage over your opponent. Today I homed in on your ignorance of the wider world to craft a successful strategy... You can't *not* recognize your loss—that would make you the child!"

"! W-well, let's play again, then! Let's play right now! I'll even take the handicap!"

"Whoops, it's almost dinnertime. Look, here comes Claire to get you. I guess I'm undefeated today!"

This time, it was the opposite of the day before: Iris insisting on a rematch, and me trying to weasel out of it.

That was how Claire found us when she came to announce dinner.

"Do you mean to win and then just ditch me?! That's no fair! Play me again! Claire, tell him! Come on, please?"

"Hey, Claire, what's good for me is good for Iris, right? Tell her to just accept her loss and eat her dinner before it gets cold! Come on, out with it! You can't let her off just because she's the princess!"

Claire was caught between us, completely lost as to what to do.

"...I'm saying, don't you ever want to leave the castle, Iris? I don't mean just to go to towns like Axel or whatever. Don't you want to see the mountains and the rivers? There are so many things we don't know about this world. You might meet a demon with a weird reputation among the local housewives or maybe a friendly Lich who only eats bread crusts."

Iris's classes went until only noon today, so we were on the terrace of her room on the top floor, drinking tea and playing a game.

"Anytime I leave the castle, a whole unit of knights comes along to keep me safe," Iris said. "And I'm not permitted to leave the capital without any attendants... Plus, there's no way there are demons or Liches like that. Please don't make too much fun of me just because you take me for a sheltered little girl... I'm teleporting to this space."

She moved one of her pieces across the board, keeping a dubious eye on me as she did so. Apparently, yesterday had taught her to keep her guard up when dealing with me.

Beside me, Lain was pouring tea into my empty cup, not participating in the conversation.

I slid my piece along the board. "You look awfully suspicious. You know, there are things in this world that don't conform to common sense. For example, normally you catch fish in the sea or in rivers, right? But did you know you can catch mackerel in fields?"

"You're lying again!"

"No, it's true! When I worked at a tavern, they told me, 'Go to the fields out back and get some mackerel!'"

"I… I think maybe they were just making fun of you…"

As Iris offered this rude remark, Lain whispered in her ear, "Your Highness, Master Kazuma isn't lying. You really can catch mackerel in fields."

"Really?! Really… I would sooner believe dogs could fly…"

"I don't know about any flying dogs," I said, "but I know a cat who breathes fire."

"This time you're definitely lying! You liar! I knew you were a liar!"

"No, seriously, it's true! It's my friend's pet!"

"M-Master Kazuma, that does strain credulity…"

"You too, Lain?! Dammit, why will no one believe me?!"

As I pounded the table in frustration, Iris said, "You let yourself get distracted, Elder Brother. Just as I planned! Looks like I win!"

And then she put me in checkmate with a girlish grin.

7

Over the course of our time together, Iris had gotten a lot better at rolling with the punches. So much so, in fact, that I started to wonder what had happened to the sincere, docile girl I'd first met. *Sheesh, I mean I'm glad she's learned to have a little fun, but I can't help feeling like I'm the butt of her jokes these days.*

And I was supposed to be a gamer, here. So how come I kept losing at our games? Maybe it was time to show her who was in charge again—if I wanted to have any hope of recovering my authority as the big brother.

It had been nearly a week since I'd come to this castle. Just as Iris had taken a shine to me, I was happily becoming accustomed to castle life.

Guess it's past noon already.

Iris would be in class until three o'clock today.

I had just woken up. I made no effort to get out of my nice, soft bed but only sat up and clapped my hands twice. The sound caused a white-haired butler in an impeccable suit to appear.

"You called, Master Kazuma?"

"Yes, I'd like my morning coffee, Sebastian."

Sebastian was my personal butler.

"I'm Heidel."

"I'd like my morning coffee, Heidel."

Apparently, Heidel was my personal butler.

Then, having asked for my coffee, I buried myself back under the covers. There should be one more person coming to take care of me sooner or later—my maid, Mary, would be in to change the sheets. But far be it from me to just get out of bed and let her change them. Making the maids' jobs more difficult was a well-accepted custom among nobles. At least, I was sure that was what Darkness had said when I was making her be my maid. And anyway, it would be a perfect way to pass the time until Iris finished her lessons.

After a while, there was a knock on the door, just as I expected.

"G'morning, Mary. If you think you're just going to waltz in here and change these sheets, you've got another think coming. Now, if you have any desire to change my bedding and get on with your work, repeat after me: 'Please, Master...'"

But it was Darkness who came into the room.

* * *

"'Please, Master,' what…? Go ahead, Kazuma, say it. Tell everyone what you had in mind." The voice belonged to Aqua, looking exasperated and following behind a shockingly serious Darkness. Megumin was with them.

"P-please, Master, give me the honor of…changing these sheets you've imbued with your fragrant aroma…"

"'Fragrant aroma'?" Darkness said. "So you still haven't lost your natural talent for sexual harassment. Hey, stop looking all embarrassed and finish your sentence! Don't you want everyone to hear?"

"F-forgive me…! What are you guys doing here anyway?! This room is supposed to be my sanctuary! Who gave you permission to come in?!" I asked defiantly.

The Crusader gave me a dark frown. "Why am I here? I'll tell you why—to take you back home! Geez, you think you can just lie around making trouble here? Let's go! Just when I think I've imagined the worst thing you can possibly do, you come up with something even more awful! Think of poor Megumin! All the sleepless nights she's spent, terrified that you were caught up in some life-threatening danger and would never come back to us!"

"I w-w-was not *that* worried! I've just had some late nights recently. Please spare me your misunderstandings!"

I wanted to interrogate the panicky Megumin a little further, but there was an even more important topic to address.

"Come home with you? As if! I'm Iris's royal playmate! And my life here at the castle is wild, and fun, and *stable*, and I'll thank you not to disturb it!"

"You moron! There's no such thing as a royal playmate! Listen up, Kazuma, and I mean listen very closely: *There is no reason for you to be at this castle.* And if you think some nobody from nowhere can just hang around at the royal castle as long as he likes, you're crazy!"

"Fine! Then I can be Iris's tutor or something! Our little princess doesn't know the first thing about the ways of the world—but I can fix that! Hey, how about you join her lessons? You're the only person I know who might be even more sheltered than she is!"

"Y-you impossible man, are you seriously—? Tutor, my ass! Lady Claire told me all about the weird influence you've been having on Princess Iris! How you do the most inappropriate things during her lessons about military affairs and strategy! How you exploit her vulnerabilities...! Unlike adventurers, royals and knights don't use dirty tricks! Don't teach her to fight like you! Come on, Aqua, say something to him!"

Darkness passed the conversation to Aqua, who came toward me angrily with her hands on her hips.

"She's right, Kazuma—it's not fair that you're the only one who gets to live in a castle! Defeating the Demon King's generals was a team effort! If you get to live in a castle, I want to live in one, too! It's only fair!"

Darkness shoved back past Aqua, who seemed to be off message. "On second thought, Aqua, don't say anything to him! You'll only make things harder."

"Oh-ho, what's this? You lost to me before—you want to challenge me again? I thought maybe you had some brains despite being a pampered little noble girl, but now I see you're not a quick study. I'm going to live my wild and fun life in this nice, *safe* castle, and you guys had better just go home if you don't want me to send you back in tears!"

"...Fine. A challenge it is, then. Everyone, please step out of the room."

Darkness was wearing only a one-piece dress. She didn't even have a weapon.

As Aqua and Megumin scuttled out of the room, I started to smile.

"Are you serious? No weapon, no armor—you really think you can win? One billowy dress is all you've got. And you know I have the ultimate antipersonnel weapon. One shot of my Steal is all it's gonna take."

"Try me," Darkness said, unimpressed. She might have thought it was a bluff.

"…Maybe you don't understand the position you're in. You're wearing next to nothing at all. If I use Steal about three times, it *will* be nothing at all. If you stop right now, I might still see my way to forgiving you—"

"I said, try me." Darkness cut me off and took a step forward.

"Y-yeah, sure. Don't joke around, okay? I'm really gonna get you."

"Then do it, if you can! It's just the two of us here! You want to strip me? Then strip me!"

Geez, she's really serious all of a sudden!

"Wait! Okay! Let's talk things out!"

"There's nothing to talk about. My mind is already made up! Some mild sexual harassment I can put up with, but you've crossed the line hoping to intimidate me! Well, do your worst! Strip me naked, attack me, whatever you want! Just do it—if you've got the nerve!"

"I knew it! I knew you were the pervy one! I'm calling you Lewdness from now on! Ahhhhhh, it's gonna break! You're gonna break it! It was a lie! I'm sorry! S-somebody help me!"

Darkness had my arm in a viselike grip. With my face smooshed into the floor, all I could do was call for help from someone outside.

The answer came from…

"U-um, Lalatina… Please…! Don't hurt him too badly…"

Apparently, Iris's lessons had ended early, and she had come to play. Now she looked at Darkness beseechingly.

Darkness had slapped her once already, yet she didn't hesitate to try to save me. My dear little sister.

"Your Highness," Darkness said, "you mustn't go too easy on this man! He's a lecherous wolf in sheep's clothing! As soon as he sees a woman, he wants to get in the bath with her or use his skills to steal her panties. That's who you're dealing with here. I'll sacrifice myself for you, Your Highness, but you must escape…!"

The moment Iris left, this girl was sure to put me through hell.

Specifically, she would flay me alive.

Well, don't assume I'll just play the underdog forever…!

Iris didn't say anything but just looked sadly at the ground.

"Erk… Y-Your Highness…"

Guess Darkness couldn't resist her, either.

I looked at Iris's downcast face and exclaimed, "Oh! See how sad you've made Her Highness? This is the most awful— Ow, ow, ow, ow, ow!"

"Quiet, you! …Your Highness, please listen to me. This man has a mansion in Axel; he's actually somewhat well-known as an adventurer. He also has friends back home, people who worry when he goes missing. I admit it—we all came here because we were worried about him. Could you please give him back to us?"

Iris still looked unhappy, but she gave a little nod.

"…I understand. I'm sorry for being so selfish…"

No! Hold your ground, Iris! Hold your ground! Don't just give in—you're the most powerful person in this castle! Throw a royal tantrum!

Iris finally managed to look Darkness in the face.

"Say, Lalatina. Maybe we could at least…throw a going-away party? Just tonight…?"

She spoke hesitantly, almost apologetically.

8

It was a royal banquet, and an especially lavish one at that.

"Hey, Kazuma, these are delicious! The organic wild melon things with ham on them? These melons are still fresh—they're practically jumping off the plates!"

"Kafuma! Kafuma! Dese ahh—*gulp*—great, too! High-quality pudding over vinegar rice, topped with wasabi soy sauce! I have no idea where this cuisine came from, but that rich sweetness and thick sauce really go together."

As I watched my companions stuff their faces at the buffet table, I realized how out of place us commoners really were.

I had changed into a suit, and the girls were wearing dresses (all borrowed from the royal wardrobe), so we looked the part. But our behavior pretty much reeked of peasantry, and the other guests obviously weren't fooled.

In one corner of the banquet hall, several hired bartenders were customizing cocktails for each guest. Aqua, apparently tired of going back for refills all the time, had simply dragged a table full of food over to the bar so she could do all her eating and drinking in one place.

Beside me, Megumin had taken a clean dish and was carefully piling food on it.

And as for the person who would normally have reined us in before things got this bad…

"Lady Dustiness, to think that one so disinterested in parties as yourself should be at an event like this—what a surprise! I'm certainly glad I showed up for the feast tonight. What a wonderful chance to see your most radiant visage!"

"Lady Dustiness, how is your father, Lord Ignis? You know, I served him for a time when I was young…"

"Ah, Lady Dustiness! I shall thank Eris, the goddess of good fortune, for my meeting you here tonight! I'd heard rumors of your beauty, but never did I imagine…!"

"The rumors don't do you the slightest justice! You outdo even the legendary Monoctus flower, which is said to bloom just once every hundred years—and the even more legendary Moongrass! Actually, I know of a store that you would like very much. Perhaps you'd let me accompany you after the party?"

"As if she would go with you! Your status is much too low to escort Miss Dustiness. Milady, you must let *me*…"

A crowd of nobles surrounded Darkness, all offering her praise ingratiating enough to set your teeth on edge. But Darkness, being noble herself, knew how to handle it; she took in everything with a polite smile while gently rebuffing the various advances.

"Thank you all so much for your kindness. It's true I'm unaccustomed to parties. I hope you'll be so kind as to understand…"

It was enough to make me want to butt in and ask who she was and what she'd done with Darkness.

She stood there playing the demure girl, but there was a slight twitch in her cheek. It looked like maybe she'd had about all she could take.

But I was surprised at how popular she was. There were lots of handsome young guys around her, all golden hair and blue eyes.

……

"So this is where you've been, Lalatina! Oh! But you're so popular, Lalatina! Well, that dress certainly does look lovely on you, Lalatina…"

I slid up next to her and started using her real name as often as I could. The shock caused her to spit out her mouthful of wine.

"*Cough!* Ack! H-how rude!" she exclaimed. As the surrounding nobles goggled at her, Darkness, her eyes swimming, dabbed at the corner of her mouth with a handkerchief. "What brings you here so suddenly, my adventurer friend Master Kazuma Satou? Calling me by that name here will leave me most distraught. I see you like your little pranks as much as ever, but you'll cause people to misunderstand the relationship between us."

Outwardly, she kept the sweet smile on her face, especially emphasizing the words *adventurer friend*.

Seriously, who is *this?*

Her words sent an obvious wave of relief through the gathered nobles.

"Ha-ha, the way he suddenly called Miss Dustiness by her first name really surprised me. Now I remember, Miss Dustiness, you're an adventurer, aren't you? Protecting the people from monsters and indulging your own preferences at the same time. Heavens, I almost took you two to have a *special* relationship…"

"You're completely right. But I'd expect no less from one of Lady

Dustiness's companions. Gifted even at joking. I admit I'm jealous of him, being able to call Lady Dustiness by her name, even in jest."

"Truly! ...On that note, Miss Dustiness, *do* you have a betrothed yet? If not, I happily offer myself as a candidate to become one of the lucky few who can call you by your first name..."

"Get in line! I've been pressing my suit with the Dustiness household for ages!"

The nobles went back to chatting up Darkness, but even as they tried to throw one another off, none of them made any attempt to leave the conversation. *I guess that's what you can expect from a bunch of powerful rich boys. They have plenty of self-confidence, and there's no end of them.*

I was just considering dropping another bomb under the guise of teasing when it happened.

"Miss Dustiness has achieved a great deal these past years. Surely there must be someone more suited to her than you lot."

This rather uncivil remark came from a man who suddenly broke into the conversation. He looked vaguely familiar. He was a big, rotund, middle-aged guy with hair everywhere except his head.

"Gracious, Lord Alderp! Such a barbed greeting..."

How could I forget that face? It was the lord of Axel, the guy who had tried to pin a crime on me and have me put to death.

"What the hell are you doing here?" I asked.

"*Y-you!*" Alderp spat. "Thanks to your dropping Destroyer's core on my mansion, my house is still under repair! I'm staying in my house here in the capital until my residence in Axel is fully rebuilt. And anyway, I'll have you remember your place, commoner! You shall address me as Lord Alderp!"

Geez, he even has a second house? He really is rich.

"Tell us, Lord Alderp. Who is this person you think would make a more suitable match for Miss Dustiness than us? Rumor says that you yourself are more than a little obsessed with her. Surely you don't think...?" said one of the nobles who had been talking to Darkness, in a voice thick with irony.

"It's not myself, of course. And not my son, either. Whatever might have once been appropriate, now, given Miss Dustiness's family status and all the things she herself has achieved, I can think of only one man who could match her."

He looked very confident about this. Just one man who could match all the things Darkness had done?

"You mean me?" I said.

"That's enough out of you! You're going to cause me nothing but trouble. Go play with Aqua and Megumin!" Darkness snapped, her facade slowly crumbling as I pushed her further and further.

Alderp ignored us; he spoke with a broad smile. "I refer to the man personally leading the army with His Majesty the king against our demonic enemies—the firstborn prince, Lord Jatice. In principle, Miss Dustiness must take a husband in order to ensure the continuation of the Dustiness family name, but if they had enough children, one of the younger ones could inherit the Dustiness household."

None of the nobles, listening silently, looked especially pleased about this.

"Prince Jatice has been fighting on the front lines for some time now, and Miss Dustiness has lately established herself with a succession of victories against generals of the Demon King. They both can already be considered heroes of our country. Being brought into the royal castle would be a fitting reward for Miss Dustiness's deeds. And I have no doubt their children would be strong and beautiful and fine. What do you all think? Are they not a most appropriate couple?"

Darkness had said this old man had an unnatural fixation on her, but he almost sounded as if he had finally given up on his unreachable flower.

"He... He's not wrong..."

"True, there would be few better matches..."

The gathered nobles began to disperse, not very enthusiastically. Darkness looked like she was about to say something...

"Hey!" I exclaimed. "So what does that make me, chopped liver? What about *us*? Lalatina, are you just going to throw me away?!"

"""""?!"""""

This drew a stunned reaction from everyone around.

"Gah, what the hell is wrong with—! Ahem, Master Kazuma, you think of the most outrageous pranks, but I believe I've already told you how much trouble your little jokes cause for me in places like this..."

Darkness smiled as she spoke, reaching out for my arm as if she were just drawing close to a friend of hers.

I dodged her neatly.

"Lalatina, think of the idyllic days we've spent together! Always living in the same house—we've even bathed together, haven't we? You washed my back, didn't you?! Why, just the other day, we played that game where you call me Master, and I—"

"Young Master Kazuma, jokes have their place, but you're really going too far!"

Darkness pursued me, no longer worried about what it looked like, reaching out for me with both hands.

"Oops! Are you sure about this, Lalatina? Do you really want all these nobles to see your beastly strength? You'll have to become a bride someday, won't you? Even though I know I'm making that hard on you. As a noble, you're reaching the age where it'll look bad if you don't get married, right? But Young Lady, if you reveal your outrageous physical strength here, you might scare off all your suit— Ow, ow, ow!"

"Goodness, ever the showman, aren't you, Master Kazuma? I'm not putting any strength into this at all, and yet your cries of pain are so believable! I wonder what they'd sound like if I really put some muscle into it. My level's gone up recently. Want to find out what I can do?"

"My joke went too far, Lady Dustiness—!"

9

I wasn't really trying to be mean, mostly. I just got a little annoyed seeing all those guys around Darkness, and I wanted to throw a wrench in the works. I didn't really want to date her myself, but I also couldn't stand the thought of a close female friend of mine belonging to someone else.

I mean, I know I was the one trying to press Darkness at a matchmaking meeting not long ago because I had my eye on the reward—but now that I didn't need the money, I found I wanted to scuttle any potential courtship.

I must admit, it was pretty selfish, even for me.

This banquet was supposed to be a going-away party for me, but with Darkness getting so much of the attention, I was all but forgotten.

It wasn't like I was eager to be the center of attention for noble guys, and I definitely wasn't feeling lonely. For some reason, all the noble ladies were firing questions at Aqua and Megumin: What shampoo did they use? What kind of soap did they like?

Well, as long as it kept them busy, that was fine.

I was *not the least bit* jealous…!

I found myself in a corner of the banquet hall, shrinking into the wall as I watched everyone make a big deal over everyone else.

"Gosh, what are you doing all the way over here?" It was Iris.

"Iris! Thank goodness, I knew I could count on you! Kind, sweet, considerate Iris! It's so *lonely* being by myself at a party like this—thank goodness I have my dear little sister, Iris!"

"G-gosh…"

My fervent praise evoked only a mutter and a blush from the princess.

Hmm? Lately, she hadn't hesitated to give me a piece of her mind over just about anything, but she was acting awfully shy today.

Her face still red, Iris lined up next to me against the wall. It looked like that obnoxious Claire wasn't following her around everywhere for now, maybe because the party was in the castle.

As she looked out at the elegant banquet hall, Iris said, "The castle will be much quieter tomorrow. Who will make Claire mad or annoy Lain?" She didn't move from the wall as she spoke.

"It's only taken a week for those two to pretty much learn to hate me. Anyway, won't the castle be better off quiet? Every day at my mansion is chaotic. If I could have one wish, it would be to live an uneventful life."

Iris glanced at me out of the corner of her eye and smiled sadly.

…Whoa. Just one little lonely gesture, and my heart starts thumping? What's with this? Am I that easy?

"I know I've treated you like a little sister basically since the moment we met, but you seem to have gotten pretty attached to me in the last week, too."

I tried to change the subject and avoid drawing attention to the fact that my pulse was racing over a twelve-year-old girl.

"Has it been a problem for you?" she asked, barely looking up at me, and my pulse only quickened.

"N-no, no way. I'm totally happy about it, you know? I just…can't imagine what would ever make anyone like me." I somehow managed to keep my voice from scratching with nervousness. Iris giggled.

Then she said, "I've never met anyone like you before. I've had lots of servants, but there was no one who was totally fearless, and rude, and obnoxious, and willing to tell a princess like me all kinds of dirty things, and who wanted to win at any cost in a totally immature way…"

"H-hey, I didn't ask you to tell me what you *don't* like about me. I was trying to find out why you *would* like me."

I was definitely getting a little confused here.

"And that's what I'm talking about, isn't it?" She smiled brightly.

Stupid, adorable princess!

Eris, Iris—why must there always be a wall between me and the sanest girls around here?

I mean, not that I saw Iris as anything more than a little sister. She was twelve years old, for crying out loud!

"By the way, about our game—I believe I won more times than you did, so it's my win overall, right?"

"The hell it is! Those later games were fifty-fifty, and if anything, when I won, my victories were by a landslide. If we could have kept playing, I definitely would have racked up more wins."

"Maybe you could finally just admit that you lost? You're being a kid right to the end, Elder Brother!"

"Well, only a kid would gloat about beating a kid in a game!"

Iris and I tired of talking after this bit of argument, both of us settling back against the wall. Sheesh, she just wasn't going to let it go, not to the bitter end.

But really, these days, Iris somehow seemed to be enjoying herself when we argued.

For a while, we didn't talk about anything. We just looked out at the party.

Over the last week, we'd talked and argued and laughed together about many things. But for some reason, standing there at that moment, we didn't do any of that. We were just silent.

Aqua and Megumin continued eating and drinking ravenously, while Darkness remained surrounded by her crowd of noble admirers.

"I'm sure I'll never forget this week I shared with you." Iris sounded almost like she was talking to herself as she watched the party. "I'm jealous of Lalatina. You all must have so much fun every day..." She sounded so lonely.

...I'm really surprised by how close we got in just a week.

I was going to go back to Axel, and starting tomorrow, this girl would have to suppress herself in order to do her duty as part of the royal family and go back to playing the good little girl who never said anything selfish.

...Isn't there some way for me to stay in the castle?

Maybe they could take me on as a knight? No, I was so pathetic that even with Iris's and Darkness's connections, it would be hard to get into a unit of knights. And when they eventually chased me out, it would be for being a bad influence on Iris and bringing no benefit of any kind to the castle.

Hmm. Maybe a general of the Demon King could conveniently attack right now? I could gallantly defeat them, and once everyone was recognizing how useful I was to have around, they wouldn't mind if I made a slightly selfish request.

I just needed to gain a bit of renown in the capital. It didn't have to be anything big. Then there might not be so much opposition to me…

As I stood there quietly fretting about this, Iris spoke up.

"I'd like to try being an adventurer, like Lalatina. The royal family has always been known for having good magical abilities and excellent training. I might not be able to be a Crusader like Lalatina… But maybe I could at least be a Wizard or a Priest? Or maybe… Maybe I could be a Thief and be like the righteous thief everyone's been talking about recently! But I guess Claire would get pretty angry if I told her I wanted to become a thief…" Then she giggled.

"Wait, what did you say everyone's been talking about?"

I raised my head suddenly, and she looked at me, surprised. "You don't know about the righteous thief, Elder Brother? As the story goes, there's a thief who breaks into the houses of evil nobles and steals all the dirty money they've made. And then the next day, a huge donation is left in front of the orphanage run by the Eris church. That's why everyone thinks this thief is on the side of justice."

A righteous thief…

"A royal like me probably shouldn't be calling someone who goes around committing theft 'righteous.' But…I think it's kind of cool, you know? Being a royal myself, I guess maybe the thief will try to steal from me sometime. But even so, I can't help admiring them a little bit."

Her eyes sparkled as she spoke. It was enough to make me jealous of this thief, and even though I had no idea what they looked like, I kind of wanted to catch them.

…Catch a thief?

"…That's iiiiit!!"

10

"Darkness! Darkness! …Oh, perfect, Claire's here, too."

"Wh-what? You again? I thought I told you to go away. I'm busy."

"D-do you need something, Master Kazuma?"

I ran up to Darkness and Claire, clearly interrupting their conversation.

"Hey, I heard this rumor! Something terrible is happening in the capital right now!"

Both of them gave me quizzical looks.

"Terrible?" Darkness said. "I guess you could call it that. Some adventurer has gotten the country's princess to start calling him 'Elder Brother.' If His Majesty finds out, don't be surprised if you end up beheaded again."

"Lady Dustiness is right," Claire added. "I have no intention of defending you in front of His Majesty when he gets back from the front lines. I'm going to tell him exactly what went on in this castle."

"That's not what I'm talking about! And anyway, I was just helping a lonely little girl pass the time while her father was away! But more importantly!" I tried to make myself as audible as possible to the other nobles. "The terrible thing I'm talking about is the righteous thief stalking the streets of the capital! I've heard! I know all the nobles who live in the capital are targets!"

"Y-yeah," Darkness said, "it does sound like that thief tends to hit nobles who are openly malicious…"

"And what about it, Master Kazuma?" Claire asked.

Confronted by two very puzzled high nobles, I jabbed my thumb at my chest. "This righteous thief everyone's talking about or whatever? I'm gonna nail 'em."

""Huh?""

Darkness and Claire looked at me blankly. The nobles nearby were clearly unnerved.

"He's going to catch the thief? The one the capital's police force and knights have been investigating but still haven't found a single clue about?"

"Who is this guy anyway? He's been hanging around the banquet hall all night. Frankly, I'm worried about him."

"Shh! He may not look like much, but I gather he's one of Lady Dustiness's companions..."

"Him?! That guy who looks more like a run-of-the-mill citizen than an adventurer?"

"Isn't he the NEET masquerading as Princess Iris's playmate? The other day, I saw him force his maid to wait out in the castle garden because he wanted to sleep until evening."

You all know I can hear you, right?

But I ignored the whispers.

"I'm, you know, I'm on pretty good terms with Darkness, and she's a noble, right? That means that for me, no matter how righteous this thief might be and no matter how popular they are as a defender of the defenseless, they're my enemy. I mean, Darkness's house could be next!"

"H-hey! My family hasn't done anything to deserve being targeted by that thief!"

Darkness tried to protest her innocence, but I balled up my fist and exclaimed, "Come on, Darkness! We've brought down generals of the Demon King—we can solve a little mystery! It must be fate that brought us to the capital! Righteous or not, stealing is stealing. We can't overlook it!"

Darkness didn't seem entirely convinced, and she fixed me with a dubious stare. "Y-you're not wrong, but... You've never had a moral compass before. Why now? What are you plotting?"

"I, uh, just thought that if I caught this thief, maybe I could hang out at the castle a little longer..."

"Wh-why, you...!" Claire sounded absolutely exasperated, but before she could finish what she was saying...

"That's wonderful!" one of the nobles exclaimed, then began clapping. One after another, the rest joined in.

"That's Lady Dustiness's companion for you! Er, not that any of us are worried about being targeted by the thief, of course…"

"I hear this man has defeated several generals of the Demon King. I'll bet he catches a dozen thieves before breakfast!"

"I, too, have no reason to fear the thief, but the capture of such a ne'er-do-well can only be good! Again: no reason for me to worry, though!"

What a transparent bunch.

…But still, this was good for me. Catching the thief would be my pretext for staying at the castle. If I actually did manage to make good on this project, I could probably stick around as long as I wanted, and I might even get a reward for my effort. And if I didn't catch the thief, well, investigations can take a long time, and I could be with Iris in the meantime.

Behind me, the princess was watching; her eyes were glittering with expectation. I never realized she was so eager to see her beloved elder brother at work! *Well, just leave it to me! After I loll about at the castle awhile longer, I'll get around to stopping that villain eventually!*

Claire looked at me, thinking about something for a moment, then she gave a nod and clapped her hands. "I see. Then here's the plan, Master Kazuma. You'll pick a noble house that seems a likely target and stay with them in order to stake out the place. If you really do manage to catch the thief, then we might be able to consider letting you stay at the castle." She turned to the nobles. "I hope all of you will cooperate with Master Kazuma's investigation!"

…Huh?

Chapter 3

May There Be Divine Punishment for This Dashing Thief!

1

Well, that didn't quite work out the way I'd planned. I had meant to prolong the investigation as much as I could, as an excuse to stay at the castle. But the next morning...

"Seriously, Kazuma! Would it kill you to go one day without getting us in trouble? Dragging us into something like this—the nerve! Well, we're in it now, so I'll help you, but you never get to complain about my behavior ever again. Ugh, so annoying. Kazumannoying!"

"She is right! You can never again call us troublemakers who only cause problems. Of course, we're comrades, so I will help you rather than abandon you!"

The two people who had done nothing but stuff their faces the night before were now lording it over me.

I hadn't asked either of them for their help, but when I tried to explain that to them, they insisted they would help anyway—no doubt in hopes of making me feel like I was in their debt.

Given that I was trying to catch a thief, I frankly didn't need either of them, but they seemed so gung ho about it that I decided to give up.

And now, we came to the number one candidate for Evil Noble House the Thief Was Likely to Hit.

*   *   *

"…and out of all the nobles in the city, you immediately came to me?"

Of course, I was talking about the second home of Axel's own despot, Alderp.

Rumor had it the targets were always the worst-behaving noble houses. And there was no end of ugly talk about this guy, so I wouldn't have been surprised if the thief showed up there.

Alderp came to the door with a bodyguard at his side, not trying to hide his displeasure, and immediately began staring openly at Darkness's body. I got it—Lewdness was lewd; I'd seen her in the bath, so I should know. But the way he was ogling her was pretty rude even by my standards.

Maybe Alderp could sense me giving him the eye, because he shot a glance my way. It seemed awfully cold somehow, but he immediately looked away again, showing no interest in me, instead focusing on Aqua. And he didn't look away from her. Aqua gave a little squeak and hid behind me.

"…My. My! I should have expected Lady Dustiness would keep such fine company! What a beauty! I could only compare you to…to a goddess!"

Aqua popped her head out from behind my back to interject. "That's no comparison—I *am* a goddess!"

"Ha-ha! Not just beautiful but funny, too!"

"Ooh, you're in for some divine punishment, mister!" Aqua shouted, but Alderp seemed to take that as a joke, too. And then his gaze turned to Megumin…

"Well now, what have we here?"

Just as I was wondering what would come out of his mouth next, the bodyguard beside him whispered something in his ear. He was far enough away to make it difficult to hear, but I could pick up snatches.

"Lord…be c…you say. She's the wiz…-ryone says is cra…"

"Her?! ...-angerous, I almost...mad!"

I saw the lord's face change color as they whispered.

"Hey! I shall have you explain your motive for looking away from me. And depending on your answer, you'll find out whether I am the person this man has been whispering to you about!"

"O-oh, it's just—you're v-very sweet, and quite lovely..."

"Oh yes? And? And?"

Alderp, cornered by Megumin, looked to me for help.

"...Hey! Don't you have any more praise for the defender of Axel Town? I think I'd better demonstrate just how powerful my explosion magic can be. I'm going to need that garden over there."

"No! I'm fully aware of the magnificence of your talents!"

...I think I'll let this play out.

"Er— Erm, Lady Dustiness, are you trying to say you believe I'm so evil as to be targeted by that thief? I was convinced you would never want to stay at my house, but I'm surprised to find you apparently hate me less than I thought. At the same time, I would have thought you were much too sophisticated to swallow a rumor hook, line, and sinker, and I would be most distraught if a bit of back-alley gossip has poisoned you against me. But if you really think I'm a likely target of that righteous thief, then by all means, stay here as long as you like." As he spouted his pseudo pleasantries, Alderp struggled to suppress a lecherous grin.

Darkness hurried to try to offer an excuse. "It's not that we suspect you of anything... This is simply, uh, a phase of the investigation..."

I pushed past her and slipped inside. "You heard the man—we can stay as long as we want! I call the biggest room!"

"No fair, Kazuma! We should discuss things like this together! I want the room that's closest to the kitchen."

"I want the highest room in the house! I do not mind even if that means staying in the attic!"

As we ran into the house one after another, Darkness was left to mutter in embarrassment, "S-sorry. They can be a lot of trouble..."

"N-not...at all... I can see it's not easy for you, either, Lady Dustiness...," Alderp replied. There was even a hint of sympathy in his voice.

According to rumor, the righteous thief we were after worked alone.

Apparently, their MO was classic Robin Hood: break in to a rich but evil noble's house, steal some money, and then give it to the orphanage. And the handful of eyewitness accounts had it that this thief was quite dashing.

Darkness muttered with a melancholy look, "What this thief is doing is a crime; it's not praiseworthy. I know it's not, and yet... Honestly, I really can't get excited about stopping this person."

We were at Alderp's mansion. I had annexed the nicest guest room as my quarters, and everyone had gathered there to work out how we were going to catch this thief.

"Uh-huh. But stealing is stealing. I hate these 'dashing' types who call themselves 'helpers of the helpless' or 'defenders of the citizenry' or whatever."

Darkness and Megumin gave me odd looks at this pronouncement.

"...Hmm. You don't exactly have such an awful face yourself. I've been wondering, do you have some kind of complex about the word *dashing*? You wanna talk about it?"

"I think you have a rather cool face, Kazuma. You needn't be so self-deprecating."

"S-stop it, you two. Why are you being so nice all of a sudden? You're gonna make me feel awfully small... What's with you, Aqua, looking all serious?"

She turned a beatific smile on me. "O wayward *hikikomori*, pray, do not criticize thyself too much. It is society's fault you're lazy, your upbringing can be blamed for your unpopularity, and your genes are at fault for your failure to flourish. No, blame not thyself but foist all responsibility onto others..."

"Aw, shaddup, I'm not being *that* self-deprecating! My appearance is one thing, but at least my personality…! Hey, stop that, why are you all giving me those weird smiles? I keep up an average appearance, at least! Stop— Stop that! Stop being nice to me!"

I pushed away the three unaccountably sweet girls and started brainstorming how to nab the thief.

Apparently, they were usually active from about midnight until dawn. My intuition, refined through battle after battle in this world, told me that they would hit this house next.

It looked like we might be here for a while.

2

It was our second day at Alderp's mansion. I had left my assigned room and was wandering the house.

This was purely in order to investigate how the thief might get in and what they might be after. I sized up the mansion from the outside, pretending I was a thief.

Hmm, that kitchen window on the first floor is looking a little worn out. Maybe Alderp was too cheap to fix it. The frame was broken; even a rank amateur could work a stake in there and pry it open.

Right. That was how I would try to get in.

I went back inside and headed for the kitchen, imagining I had just broken in. Any invader would probably come late at night, so the hallway would be completely dark. The Second Sight skill was available only to Archers and Adventurers, so the thief would be feeling their way in the dark, moving slowly along the wall…

As I followed the probable path, running this "thief simulation" in my head, I came to a snug little room. It didn't look likely to have anything in it, but if I were a thief, I'd want to be sure. With that in mind, I opened the door…

"Hrm? Oh, it's you. There's nothing in this room. Even if you don't have anything to do, don't just go wandering around the house."

Inside, I found Alderp.

Like he said, there was nothing there, just a big mirror hanging on the wall.

But then, what was he doing there?

Then I saw the bucket and towel in Alderp's hands. He must have been cleaning the room.

Wait, isn't that usually the servants' job...?

As I pondered this, a new figure appeared in the mirror on the wall.

"Huh? What's with this mirror? Is it some kind of magical item? Like, a magic mirror?"

It was a maid.

The next room over, it seemed, was the bath, which the maid was cleaning. I looked right at her, but she showed no sign of noticing me.

...Hang on a second.

"Hey, old man. You're not really polishing that mirror, are you?"

He looked away uncomfortably. "You... You want to look with me...?"

"You think I'd agree to something like that? Did you buy this mirror specifically because Darkness was staying here? I mean, as a man, I understand, but... There has to be a line somewhere. I'll keep this place a secret from my friends, but in exchange, you can't use it while I'm here, okay? And just to be sure, I think I'll sleep in this room. Come on, out, out, out!"

I made a shooing motion at Alderp. His shoulders slumped sadly, and he started for the door...

...but then he stopped.

"Wait... But that means..."

"Nuh-uh, stop right there! I don't want any nasty little misunderstandings. I'm not like you! I'm doing this to protect my friends!"

"Then there's no need to sleep here! It would be enough to keep an eye on me while your friends were bathing. *You* get out of here! I wouldn't expect a brat like you to have the proper reverence for Lalatina's naked form!"

"I hate to break it to you, but Darkness and I have already bathed together! But either way, I don't plan to waste my valuable time keeping watch on you. You want me to tell Darkness—let alone your maids—that you have a room like this? I'm just trying to keep everybody happy, so if you don't want every lady in the house to hate you, just keep your mouth shut!"

"You want to tell the maids? Go ahead! I pay them very generous salaries—and besides, they're maids! A bit of sexual harassment comes with the job! But let me tell you—*what* bodies they have! Sure you're not interested? How about *I* propose a little trade? I can tell we're of a kind, you and I; I can smell it on you. We're just two men who both want to be happy."

"Are… Are their bodies really that great…?"

"Indeed! Greater than great!"

A moment passed. Then I silently extended my hand, and Alderp reached out to shake it…

"Consider my interest piqued. I shall have you tell me what is so great."

Just as we were about to shake, a familiar voice came from the door. I hurriedly pulled my hand back.

We didn't need to look to see who it was. Alderp and I both pointed at each other and exclaimed:

""He was trying to peep at…!""

And so the magic mirror was shattered.

Three days had passed since we'd come to guard the house. There had been no sign of the thief yet; our lives went on peacefully, pretty much the way they had in Axel.

Aqua and Darkness had been taking frequent trips out ever since they got to the capital, and I didn't see much of them around the house. Aqua swore she was going to drive out the Eris Church, which was doing pretty well for itself around here, so she was off being annoying under the guise of evangelism.

As for Darkness, the nobles at the castle had invited her to come and get to know them a little better the past several days.

And me?

"Oh, Kazuma, good morning. Although, it is already past noon."

Megumin greeted me as I came into the dining area just after waking up. She was having lunch.

"I'm up late every night watching for that thief," I said. "I'm not just living a dissolute life. And anyway, I recall hearing you hardly slept yourself while I was away."

"?! W-well, I— Yes, I was awake rather late those nights! But I got up early anyway! More to the point, do you think the thief will show up soon?!" She seemed a little panicky. She held a piece of half-eaten bread in her hand.

What is this, some kind of romantic comedy?

"What are you so worked up about? Does this mean Darkness was right? Were you *worried* about me? What a surprisingly sweet side of you…" I smirked teasingly at her, and Megumin blushed faintly.

"I… Yes, I suppose I was worried. You're so weak, but you get yourself into trouble so easily. And you don't get yourself right back out of it, like the main character in some story. Instead you just get killed."

"I-it's not like I enjoy getting myself into trouble or dying! Hey, quit it, when you turn thoughtful like that all of a sudden, how am I supposed to know what to do?!"

This unexpected counterattack threw me off. Megumin just giggled.

"And after all the things I tried back at the village… Kazuma, you can be rather meek and mild yourself." Then she grinned, as if she was getting payback for my teasing her.

Grr! It's not like she has any romantic experience, either, so how is she so able to mess with me?

Come to think of it, what even were we to each other right then? When Megumin said she "liked" me, what did that mean? If I took it at face value and said I *liked* her, too, she might have been all, *I didn't mean like that, I meant I liked you as a friend...*

I remembered how annoyed I used to get with characters in manga or light novels in Japan, where it was obvious they were in love, and readers would be like, *Just notice each other already! Pick up the pace!*

But now I was actually in such a situation, and it was a lot more complicated than I'd thought.

I hesitated to take a step forward, afraid of shattering the pleasant relationship we'd had until now. I mean, *did* I even really like her that way?

Adolescent men are simple creatures. Hold their hand or show the slightest sign of interest, and they'll be head over heels in the blink of an eye.

While I sat fretting, Megumin finished her food. "Kazuma, once you're done with breakfast, will you go on a date with me?"

It was as simple as that. And then she smiled.

Megumin's voice rang out across the mountain range near the capital.

"*Exploooooosion!!*"

This was about what I expected!

When Megumin had asked me on that date, I set about looking for somewhere outside the capital she could let off an explosion.

"Look!" Megumin exclaimed. "Did you see that? What an explosion! The power! The area of effect! Another brilliant display!"

"Uh-huh, great stuff. Ow! Hey, keep it under control—I can't give you a piggyback ride with you thrashing around like that!"

"Reprimand me if you must, but I just reduced a mountain to pebbles!"

Ever since we had gotten back from Crimson Magic Village,

Megumin's passion for her explosion magic had gotten even more intense. Now that I had dumped all the skill points she'd been saving into strengthening Explosion, her blasts had gotten powerful enough to present a genuine threat to humankind.

For the residents of Axel, the roar of her once-daily explosion had become part of the scenery; nobody batted an eye at the sound. But the same wasn't true of the capital, and apparently, a lot of people had been complaining to Alderp.

Actually, even though she'd been in the capital for only a few days, Megumin already seemed to be gaining a reputation.

Ever since I'd made those changes to Megumin's Adventurer's Card back at the village, all her anxiety seemed to have disappeared, and she'd completely stopped doubting herself. I wondered why I'd decided to do that.

With Megumin riding on my back, I sighed and muttered, "I probably *should* have had her learn advanced magic…"

"I believe you just said something I cannot overlook! Your words and actions that day were so full of emotion, and now—!"

She jabbered on as I got us home to Alderp's mansion.

One week since we came to the mansion.
Still no thief.

"Just a minute! Don't underestimate the goddess of water—you can't fool me when it comes to wine! I know there was a nice, expensive bottle in the library! Well, hurry up and get it for me!"

That was Aqua, who in the previous week had managed to drink Alderp's house dry.

"…and my explosion blew him to pieces! That pitiful Demon King General Hans was reduced to cinders! And after *that* was the battle with Demon King General Sylvia. Let me tell you how I acquitted myself…"

Megumin was cornering not just the maids but even Alderp himself, trapping them for half a day at a time with stories of her heroism. And as for me…

"Miss Maid! Oh, Miss Maid! I believe it's time for my massage! Oh, and for dinner tonight I want white ox sukiyaki. And the king-size bed and fluffy blankets I ordered will be arriving soon, so set them up in my room!"

I had made myself completely at home.

Recently, the lot of us had taken to spending our days leisurely in the parlor together. Since we couldn't go back to the castle, I would be just as happy if this place remained at risk for the rest of our lives.

And there was Alderp, watching us vacantly, possibly having gotten a little thinner over the past few days. In a tired voice, he said, "Lady Dustiness…"

At that, Darkness, who was huddled in a corner of the parlor, jumped.

"I know I told you to stay here as long as you needed to, but…"

"You don't have to say anything more! I'll get them out of here right away!" Darkness hung her head, looking ready to weep from embarrassment.

3

It had gotten to be around two or three o'clock in the morning…

"Well, crap… I was *sure* they were gonna hit this house…"

The ones who were the most active around this time were the undead and NEETs.

I found myself unable to sleep because of the generous nap I'd taken during the day, so I wandered down to the kitchen, feeling peckish.

This could be a problem. Everyone hated Alderp so much. What was that thief doing not showing up? I had been so sure that I would catch them here and that the subsequent improvement in my reputation would get me back into the castle…

But we were supposed to leave this mansion tomorrow, so that would be the end of my stakeout.

Had the thief figured out we were there? And wasn't I supposed to be really lucky? What happened to that? Come to think of it, from what

I'd heard, I gathered Lady Eris was the goddess of good fortune. Maybe that was it. Darkness was an Eris follower. Maybe I'd teased her too much and upset the goddess.

Or maybe that thief just had even better Luck than I did...

When I got to the kitchen, I realized someone was in there. I could sense their presence, but there were no lights on. Which, at this time of night, could only mean...

...it was Aqua, who could see even better in the dark than I could and kept similar hours to mine. I was sure she was there looking for a snack to go with her drinks. I was just about to call out when someone started talking to themselves in the dark, very quietly.

"They're not even keeping watch? Maybe I overthought this... But I've been avoiding this room because of the bad feeling it gives me..."

The last night before we were supposed to leave, and it looked like we finally got something. Thank you, Eris, goddess of good luck!

"Hmm...? Did I just sense something strange...?"

Whoops! We were dealing with a righteous thief here—I was sure they belonged to the Thief class. That meant they might be able to detect me using a skill like Sense Foe. I had unconsciously activated Ambush, counting on it to keep me hidden as I stuck close to the wall and stayed perfectly still in the darkness.

"Just my imagination...?"

The intruder began to shuffle through the dark room. They had to grope their way along, which meant I'd been right about them not having any skills that let them see in the dark. I came up behind the thief, closing the distance, when I noticed something.

"Okay, Sense Treasure, go! ...Hmm, looks like it's over here..."

Whoever heard of a thief who talked to themselves so much?

"Gotcha!"

"?!"

As I grabbed hold of the intruder, my hands cupped something soft.

That's right: This thief was a woman.

"Okay, come quietly! Bwa-ha-ha-ha-ha! You picked the wrong guy to mess with, you dirty thief! You might have tricked those other morons, but I've gone head-to-head with several generals of the Demon King—I'm not letting some crook get away!"

"Stop! Hang— Hang on! Hey, wait, that voice—"

Huh?

You know, this thief did sound kind of familiar.

"Kazuma, is that you?! Hrk! You know, you could probably stand to grab a less compromising part of me!"

"I'm just trying to restrain an intruder. Wait…" My night vision didn't allow me to see faces clearly, but I realized who this was.

"It's me! Darkness's friend—the one who taught you some skills…!"

The intruder was none other than Chris, trying to hide her identity with a bandanna around her face.

4

I reluctantly let go of Chris. I pulled out the lighter I'd gotten at Wiz's shop, and the faint light illuminated Chris, hugging herself and with tears pooling in her eyes.

"*Sniff…sniff…* Your hands were everywhere… How can I ever become a bride now?"

"Well, what did you want me to do? I thought you were a thief! I don't have any good skills to restrain you with. Go ahead, take me to court. I'm sure I'll win."

"I can teach you a useful skill called Bind later…"

I took another look at the sniffling Chris. She was wearing black leggings and a black shirt and even had a black cloth tied around her mouth. Of course, if she was sneaking into someone's house wearing a getup like that…

"So you're the righteous thief everyone's been talking about, huh?"

"I sure am. Hey, what are you doing here anyway?"

I gave her the short version. Chris scrunched up her face.

"Y-you mean Darkness is here?! Aww, no, this is bad! If she finds out I'm doing stuff like this, she'll be really angry!"

"What else would you expect? Even a righteous thief is still robbing people. Anyway, Darkness likes you. If you just apologize, she probably won't have you killed. What's wrong is wrong. Own up to what you've done and pay the price."

"Hold on! You're making a big mistake; I swear there's a reason for this!"

Of course she had her reasons. But I had mine, too. Right now, I needed to do something heroic.

Besides, since she was Darkness's friend, it would probably make it harder to punish her. All the nobles she stole from had made their money illicitly anyway, and no one would want a big public trial. If she played her cards right, I figured Chris could get off with an out-of-court settlement.

As I was busy thinking about all this, I heard something coming our way. I guess we'd made too much noise.

Chris looked up at me from where she was sitting on the floor, appearing to have made up her mind. "Looks like I don't have a choice. I'll tell you what's really going on. If we explain everything to Darkness, I'm sure she'll understand—she'll probably even help!"

Those resolute eyes gave me a very bad feeling. I knew what was coming next.

"I have a good reason for breaking into these nobles' houses and stealing from them…"

It was what always came next: I would get stuck in yet another dangerous escapade!

"No, stop right there; I don't want to hear it! And you don't have to tell Darkness, either!"

Chris looked perplexed by this outburst. But I knew Darkness. She was so dense, if she heard that something bad was happening, she could never let it go. I wanted to do something heroic, yes, but even more than that, I wanted to do something *safe*. And wherever this conversation was going, it would more than likely involve danger.

"Huh? B-but…"

"Nope! Come on, run away before someone gets here! I'll pretend I never saw you!" I started shoving Chris toward the kitchen.

"Wh-what? But I…I really want your help…"

"La-la-la, I can't hear you! Anyway, think about it! There's a disgusting lecher of a lord heading this way! If he sees a female thief here…"

"C-consider me gone, for today! I'll find another chance to tell you what's going on!"

"No, don't come back! I-in fact, use Bind on me! Then I'll have an excuse for how you got away!"

"G-good call! Here goes—*Bind*!"

Chris pulled out a rope and invoked the skill, and my body was tied up. Then she scampered away, out the kitchen window and into the night.

"Kazuma, are you okay?!"

The first person to arrive was Darkness, carrying a lantern. Aqua and Megumin were close behind her.

"Oh no…!" Megumin exclaimed. "Someone hit Kazuma with Bind! What happened to the thief?!"

"I almost had him—but he got away! He got me when my guard was down…!" I did my best to look genuinely frustrated in my predicament.

"So he got away. Still, it's not your fault. This person has hit one heavily guarded noble mansion after another and has still never been caught. I'm more worried about you. Are you hurt? What kind of person are we dealing with here?" Darkness knelt beside me and tried to loosen the bonds, but because these ropes were created by the Bind skill, it couldn't be done.

"The thief was a guy in a weird mask. He was crazy quick—I'll bet he could get the drop on one of the Demon King's generals if they weren't careful."

"Th-this must be quite the opponent—!" Megumin started, shocked.

Then Aqua, who hadn't said anything until that moment, slipped up close to me and knelt down. "...By the way, Kazuma. You look kind of like you're in a cocoon... Can you move at all?"

"What do you think? I almost had that thief cornered, but then he used Bind on me. Hey, you can't get rid of it with your magic or something, can you? I know you can break spirit barriers and stuff."

"Who do you think I am? Of course I can do it." She was smiling.

"That's my Aqua, always coming through when it counts! Hurry up and untie me, then. It sucks not being able to move." I asked Aqua—who was being a little friendlier than usual—for her help, but at the same time I had a bit of a bad feeling.

"Hey, Kazuma. I know it's kind of an awkward time, but I'd like to apologize to you…"

"…For what? Spit it out."

Okay, now it was a *really* bad feeling.

"Well, you see… Since you didn't come back from the castle for so long, I messed up your room just to kill time. And, uh… That figure, or whatever it was, that you were making? It kind of broke when I played with it."

Now I was spoiling for a fight. When I got out of those ropes, she was gonna get it. But at the moment, I didn't exactly have the upper hand. There wasn't much I could do.

"H-hey, whatever. I can make another one. Just say you're sorry, and it's water under the bridge. But first, hurry up and untie me…"

"You'll forgive me? Great! In that case, I've got lots more to confess. Let me get it all off my chest now. Actually, I figured since no one

was using your room anyway, I would do some drinking there. I mean, when I drink in my room, it's such a pain to have to clean up the bottles and the leftover snacks when I'm done, right? So I got a little drunk and…broke some other stuff, too." Her face, but not her voice, seemed apologetic as she chirped, "Sorrrrry!"

Oh, she'll pay…

Apologizing while I was immobilized? What a dirty move! But if I gave her a piece of my mind then, while I still couldn't move, there was no telling what she might do to me.

"D-don't worry about it. We're friends, right? It was my fault for not coming home! So now that your conscience is clear, you can—"

But Darkness and Megumin shoved Aqua aside.

Darkness: "Oh! I've just realized…"

Megumin: "…how much fun we can have with him like this!"

The lantern illuminated their devious grins.

Alderp heard the commotion and came running into the dim kitchen with his bodyguard.

"What in the world is going on?! Has the thief broken—? Wait, what *is* going on here?!"

No sooner had he come in than he saw me and stopped.

As soon as I saw him, I cried, "Help meee!"

Darkness was looking down at me, really enjoying herself. "No, not 'Help meee!' I told you, say 'I'm sorry for being so high and mighty recently! I'm sorry for causing you nothing but trouble! I'm sorry for embarrassing you over and over!'"

"I'm sorry! I'm sorry for causing you trouble! I'm sorry for embarrassing you!"

"I want to hear you say those words again—those cool words you said before! So tell me: How many points was my explosion?"

"Stop it! That's something I can only say once! Don't try to get me to say it again; it's embarrassing!"

"No, it's not! Go ahead, say it—come on, don't be shy!"

"Bwa-ha-ha-ha-ha! I think I like being in control every once in a while! Now, next you're going to say…"

With tears in my eyes, I turned toward the man I had once hated and begged for his help.

"Lord Alderrrrrp!!"

5

The next morning.

We'd come to the castle to report what had happened the night before. We were in a room deep in the building called the audience chamber.

Claire was speaking, and she was none too happy with me.

"I see. So after all that boasting, you were thwarted by a simple Bind skill?"

On the throne at the far end of the audience chamber, in place of the king, who was away on campaign, sat Iris.

I could hardly admit that the thief was an adventurer we knew, so I made up a fictional villain: a masked master burglar.

"Well, I'd hardly call it a complete failure! If I hadn't been there, Old Man Alderp might be a lot poorer right about now!"

That set the nobles talking. I was surprised how many people seemed to be saying that that might not have been such a bad thing.

"…Hmm. Very well. These are the words of the great Kazuma, conqueror of the Demon King's generals. I'm sure there's no need to bring in a magical lie detector. Yes, this thief must have been quite the opponent."

She didn't exactly sound like she believed me.

Behind me, I could feel Megumin prickle at Claire's sarcastic response. Darkness hurriedly put a stop to whatever Megumin had been about to do. Iris rose from her throne.

"Ahem… In any case, excellent work! You didn't fail at captur-ing the thief—you succeeded at preventing a burglary. You deserve no blame!" Her face was red, and her little fist was clenched.

I thanked her silently.

With a disturbed expression, Claire said, "Such is the generosity of Princess Iris. You gave your word, in front of many nobles, that you would accomplish a task, and yet you failed. Normally that would war-rant punishment. You should be grateful for the princess's mercy." She paused. "But since you failed to capture the thief, there's no reason for you to stay at the castle. Now get out!"

As we worked our way out of the castle, the maids and butlers we encountered acted cold toward us. Apparently, they'd gotten word of my failure. Now everyone knew that I was nothing special.

"Ehhh, don't worry about it," Darkness said. "You did good. Just like Princess Iris said, you did manage to keep the thief from stealing anything. Come on, let's go home. I won't even bug you to find work for a while. We're going to get a windfall from Vanir, right? Let's kick back."

"Have you had your fun, Kazuma?" Megumin asked. "Let's go back to Axel. We can lounge around our mansion just as well as this castle, right?"

They were trying to comfort me. And even I wasn't exactly married to the idea of being a NEET in this castle. What bothered me was Iris, who, despite being just a twelve-year-old kid, had to work so hard never to seem self-indulgent. The thought of her all by herself in this huge castle wouldn't stop eating at me.

But the difference in our social status was huge, and even if I stuck around the capital, there was no telling whether I could be any use to her. I hated to say it, but I had run out of cards to play.

I looked back at the looming castle and sighed, keenly aware of my own powerlessness.

"…Yeah. I guess we'd better go home."

Darkness and Megumin looked relieved. What, were they afraid I'd get caught up in something else if I stayed here in the capital?

"Hey, Kazuma, how about we wait until tomorrow to go home? I want to buy souvenirs. There's lots of good wine in the capital. Hey, you don't have anything else to do, right? Come shopping with me!"

There went Aqua, as oblivious to the mood as ever.

6

"The wines around here aren't so great. Michael's shop in Axel has better stuff."

"Who the hell is Michael? And you're starting to cozy up to the locals, aren't you? A little while ago, the butcher came by with a top cut of meat. He said it was for 'healing an injury.'"

Aqua had muscled me, and me alone, into accompanying her on her shopping trip. I had sent Darkness and Megumin to find us somewhere to stay tonight.

I wished the thoughtless Aqua would learn a thing or two from Iris, who was so well loved by everyone around her.

"Hey, that's the first I've heard about that. I don't remember getting any meat…"

"You and Megumin happened to be out at the time. Darkness and I hadn't had lunch yet, so she cooked it up and we ate it."

I was just fending off a physical assault from Aqua when someone called out from behind us.

"Oh? Lady Aqua, fancy meeting you here!"

Standing there was a weirdo I hadn't seen in a long time: the Sword Master, wielder of an enchanted blade. He came from Japan, just like me, and I was pretty sure his name was…Matsurugi, right?

I was used to seeing him with a girl on each arm, but today he was alone.

Aqua sounded a bit confused. "Wh-who are you again?"

She was the one who had sent him here, and she had already forgotten he existed.

Matsurigi seemed to think this was funny. "You always did love jokes, didn't you, milady?"

Aqua, however, was trying to hide behind me. She whispered in my ear, "Hey, Kazuma, who is this person? He seems to think he knows me…"

"U-um, it's me, milady. You chose me to save this world and gifted me a magic sword. I'm a Sword Master. My name is—"

"His name is Katsuragi," I said. "Don't you remember him?"

"K-Katsuragi?! I'm Mitsurigi! You could at least remember my name!" He was shouting so loud, a vein stood out on his forehead.

The name didn't seem to be jogging Aqua's memory. It had been a while since we'd talked, but we had at least seen him around, like at the battle with Destroyer.

"Not ringing any bells? He's the guy with the enchanted sword Gram?"

Aqua clapped her hands as if she'd finally remembered. Even Mitsurugi seemed to realize at this point that she wasn't being funny but had actually forgotten him.

"S-say, Kazuma Satou… You didn't really forget my name, did you? Tell me, what's my first name…?"

"I really don't think we're friendly enough to be on a first name basis yet."

"It's Kyouya! If you don't remember, just say so! Kyouya Mitsurugi! And I'll thank you to remember it this time!" he shouted, sounding more and more agitated. He put his hands to his temples and shook his head. Finally he let out a sigh, as if he had calmed down somewhat. "…Sheesh. I see I'll have to settle things with you. I've gotten stronger since we last met. I won't let you get away with your dirty tricks this time! Now face me again!"

"What are you talking about? Things *are* settled. We fought; I won. I'm not going another round with you. I beat you when I was a total newb. Just accept it and move on."

"You…"

He almost looked sad, but I knew that if I went fair and square against an advanced class with a magic sword, I had no hope of winning.

After a moment, Mitsurugi sighed. "…Never mind. Actually, I'm glad I ran into you. It's perfect timing. We need to talk."

All of a sudden he looked very serious.

Aqua and I sat down at one of the capital's many cafés to talk with Mitsurugi. Once we had placed our orders, he put his hands on the table and leaned forward slightly.

"Let's start from the top… Well, first I have something I want to give to Lady Aqua."

He took out an object. It was a small package in cute wrapping paper.

…*Oh?*

He put it in front of Aqua, who was industriously folding her napkin into something artistic.

"Lady Aqua. I don't think I ever see you wearing any accessories. And let me say, your beauty is in no way diminished by their absence… But if you'd like, please accept this…" It was enough to set my teeth on edge. I'd bet this guy wasn't a gamer back in Japan. I'd bet he actually *enjoyed* off-line life.

"What's that? You're giving this to me?"

"Yes, milady. It's just a cheap bauble; I worry that it won't suit your exalted tastes…" He had a soft smile on his face. What a smooth operator.

It made me sick.

"Hey, where's your arm candy?" I asked. "You send 'em away so you can flirt a bit?"

"They aren't my arm candy; they're my valued companions! And right now, they're off raising their levels in the next country. I tend to dominate the hunting when we go out together, you see. I put a stop to the Demon King each time he tries something here."

Aqua ignored us and opened her gift. It turned out to be a small ring. It sure didn't look cheap—it was really classy, in fact. I guess Mitsurugi was just being humble. But how did he know Aqua's ring size?

Just as I was thinking this...

"...? It's too small—it doesn't fit." Aqua had tried a couple of times to get it on her finger and had quickly given up.

Mitsurugi gave a wry smile. "The ring is enchanted. The size should—"

But he was interrupted by Aqua exclaiming, "Kazuma, Kazuma, look at this!" She covered the ring with her napkin. "Ta-daa!" She pulled away the napkin, and the ring was gone without a trace.

"...Wow. That's really neat, but where did the ring go?" I asked her.

"...Huh? I made it disappear. How should I know where it goes?"

"Uhhh," Mitsurugi said dumbly.

Gee... I feel a little bad for him.

"It may have been a cheap thing that didn't fit, but at least I was able to get a good magic trick out of it. Thanks!" Aqua gave him an innocent, carefree smile. Mitsurugi could barely speak.

"B-but of course...! I'm thrilled to have assisted in your magic trick..." He gave a dry laugh.

Gee... I feel really *bad for him.*

Aqua went back to folding her napkin, humming as if nothing had happened. Mitsurugi looked at her with a mix of adoration and pity, then turned to me.

"Okay, let's talk. This involves you, too, even if you don't know it."

In summary: The reason Beldia, the general of the Demon King, had been sent to Axel in the first place was that the king's prophets had spoken of a great light descending in that area. The king sent Beldia to investigate, not quite sure whether to believe it or not. Then Beldia was killed, and Vanir, who followed him, went missing. Sylvia, the general who had attacked Crimson Magic Village, had been finished off, too.

Apparently, there was a rumor making the rounds in the Demon King's army that a particular party of adventurers had somehow been involved in each of these incidents. The Demon King was now rather interested in that party. It was possible he would attack Axel, the town where these adventurers had their base, or he might send another subordinate.

And I had a sinking feeling that the adventurers in question were my party members and me.

"But what about that 'great light' that supposedly descended around Axel?"

I nonchalantly looked over at Aqua, who sat beside me diligently working on something. Mitsurugi followed my glance.

"I think it was Lady Aqua," he said. "Though I once wondered if this light that so alarmed the Demon King might have been myself... D-don't look at me like that..."

He had noticed my *This guy has the best misunderstandings* stare and frowned in annoyance.

As we exchanged facial expressions, Aqua said, "Done!" Then she said to Mitsurugi, "Here, you can have this. To thank you for that ring. The title of this piece is *Goddess Transformer Eris*. Her chest armor comes on and off and allows for up to three different transformations."

She handed the napkin to Mitsurugi, but I'd be damned if anyone understood what she was going on about. He took it with a strained smile.

"Ha-ha, thank you very much, Lady Aqua. I'll take good care of—"

""Whoa!""

As he spoke, he looked down at the napkin. He and I both noticed it at the same time. The folded napkin really did look like Lady Eris. It was way beyond simple origami; it could only be called art.

"...Hey, Aqua, make one of these for me, too."

"No way, I never make the same thing twice. How about a *Martial Arts Action General Winter*? I could make that for you."

"Uh, okay, sure. Yes please."

Aqua silently set to work folding another napkin. The sight caused Mitsurugi to stand up, smiling.

"Kazuma Satou. Kindly look after Lady Aqua until I get a little bit stronger." He turned to her. "With that, Lady Goddess, I must be going. I will treasure this napkin creation."

Aqua looked up at him with a *Huh?* "...? Oh, sure. Catch you next time... Hey, Kazuma, you're sure you want it to transform, right?"

"Obviously! Who wouldn't?"

Mitsurugi looked at us, almost sadly. "You and Lady Aqua really are a good match, aren't you?"

And then, with a word of farewell, he left us.

On the way back to our inn...

"You know, I feel like that's the first time in a while anyone has called me 'goddess.' That Katsuragi isn't such a bad guy."

If you really think that, you could at least remember his name.

Although it was also sort of my fault for calling him Katsuragi in the first place.

I looked at Aqua, obliviously spouting BS, and thought: *The Demon King is worried about this ditz?*

...He couldn't be.

Nope, definitely not.

"Never mind," I said. "What do you want for dinner? The capital area is more of a battleground than Axel, so apparently you can get fresh meat from stronger monsters. And all the inns here use the freshest ingredients they can, so you get a meal that's delicious and earns you lots of experience points. I feel like having something really rich. Let's buy some kind of expensive meat and grill it up."

"Me, I want something nice and light. Raw vegetables, maybe some seared meat. Something that would go with a strongish wine."

"Okay, let's play a game to decide. But Mitsurugi reminded me you're a goddess, so I'll give you a special handicap. Three rounds of rock, paper, scissors, and if you win even one of them, we'll eat what you want."

"Oh, what's this? How generous of you, Kazuma. With a setup like that, we might as well not even play! But oh well. Here goes! Rock—paper—"

She may have been a goddess, but she totally lacked the ability to learn, which meant she'd forgotten that I'm an extremely good rock, paper, scissors player. I went back to the inn carrying a cut of top-quality meat.

7

That night.

I had been asleep in my bed, but I was suddenly awakened by the sense that someone was there.

"…up… Wake up, already…!"

The voice was familiar. In the dark, I could just make out someone beside my bed.

"Perverrrrt!"

"Ahhh! Hey! It's me! It's Chris! Stop—what do you think you're grabbing? Stop it! Darkness! Darkness, help meeee!"

Once I had apprehended the intruder, I realized it was just Chris.

"Oh, it's you, Chris. If you're sneaking in here in the middle of the night, I'm assuming you don't want everyone to know what you've come to talk to me about. So why call to Darkness for help?"

"Y-you're impossible! I'm pretty sure you only grabbed the 'intruder' *after* you knew it was me! And if you're just trying to hold someone down, you don't have to grab them *there*, do you?!"

Chris was breathing hard in the darkness. I had thought our Crusader might come running when she heard the commotion, but it didn't seem like anyone had woken up.

"Geez, I really can't let my guard down with you… As much as

I really, really hate to have to rely on you of all people, I don't have a choice."

"Hey, you're the one who practically crawled into my bed in the middle of the night and then shouted when I grabbed you. What are you trying to do, set me up?"

"I didn't crawl into your bed! And I'm not trying to set you up! I told you I would come explain why I was breaking into houses, didn't I?! H-hey! Stop pretending you can't hear me!"

Chris grabbed onto me. I had my hands over both my ears and was trying to bury myself back under my covers.

"I told you back at Alderp's mansion that I didn't want to know, didn't I?! I'm already angry about being kept away from the princess, so come back some other time. Like maybe next year!"

"It has to be now! Come on, listen to me! I swear there's a reason I'm breaking into these nobles' houses…!"

I was still deep under my covers and continuing my attempts to resist, but Chris started explaining anyway…

In this world, there were exceptionally powerful magical items and equipment called "Sacred Treasures." As the name implied, they were not easy to get your hands on. But the people who did have them tended to share a few personal characteristics. They usually had black hair and black eyes and weird names.

"In other words, people with weird names like yours are usually the only ones who can get Sacred Treasures."

"My name is weird? You're acting like I'm a member of the Crimson Magic Clan or something."

My resistance had been in vain; the pillow I had stuck my head under had been torn away, and now I was listening to Chris explain something that didn't make a lot of sense to me.

I had heard about divine items from Aqua. In fact, I had seen a catalog of them—they were the overpowered "cheat items" I could have picked from when I came to this world.

"As it happens, two such items lost their owners—I don't know how. But apparently, a certain noble bought them."

"I see."

According to her, the owners of the divine items had died, and their possessions had become fair game. One of these items summoned a random monster, which could then be controlled without paying any additional cost. The other allowed you to trade bodies with another person.

Being able to control a monster sounded like a powerful ability, and I could understand why someone might want it. But who had brought the body-switch item here—and what had they planned to do with it?

As I sat wondering about this, Chris was swinging her legs from the edge of the bed. "So one of my thief skills is Sense Treasure, which lets me know when there's rare loot around. I'm using that skill to search every house in the capital."

"And you think the only people with the spare cash to buy something like a Sacred Treasure are nobles who got rich illegally?"

"Yes, exactly! But once I got in, I didn't find the divine item. I've always wanted to be a noble thief, so I helped myself to a bit of their dirty money!"

So she basically decided to turn Robin Hood on the spot?

"That mansion you were staying in sent my treasure sense off the charts. That's why I snuck in there."

"I get it. At least, I get why you were breaking into people's houses. I still don't know what you want with those Sacred Treasures, though."

Chris scratched the scar on her cheek with a hint of embarrassment. "Why I'm after those divine items…? Well, maybe I can tell you, eventually. Anyway, did you see any treasure in that mansion that might fit the bill? That old guy, Alderp or whoever, did you see him use any amazing magical items?"

"He had a magic mirror that let him see into the bath. But other than that, no, no awesome magical items… Wait, are you sure the treasure you were sensing wasn't Aqua's feather mantle? She claimed that was once a divine item."

That completely took the wind out of Chris's sails. "W-well, maybe, then… But look, there's a reason I snuck in here, too."

I knew it!

"No way! I don't want to get caught up in any more dangerous escapades! And everything you've said sounds plenty dangerous already!"

"Hey! No, hear me out! Listen, I sense a major treasure at the castle, too. One at least as big as what I sensed at Alderp's mansion!"

"I think it's pretty common for castles to have treasure in them. So what?"

"As I recall, you have the Second Sight skill, don't you? You can see in the dark! And I know I taught you Ambush and Sense Foe. With those abilities, you and I can sneak in—"

"I'm not gonna be your accomplice! I've had a bad feeling ever since I ran into you at Alderp's mansion. No way am I helping you with this!"

"Don't say that! I'm not done yet! If we don't get this Sacred Treasure, it's going to spell trouble for everyone!"

"Well, if it's that important, I think you'd better get in touch with an actual hero, then! Hey, I've got a thought. There's a guy name Mitsurugi in town. If you tell him a missing Sacred Treasure is going to fall into the wrong hands and be used for evil, you'll have him at hello!"

"You coward! I want *you* to do it! Fine! I'll go wake up Darkness and ask her!"

"Hey, stop! Darkness is a noble, too. If the other nobles find out you're the thief, she could be in real trouble!"

"But I—"

"Just get out of here already! Go home, or I'll use that Bind skill I learned from you last night, and then you'll find out what sexual harassment really means! Incidentally, that little ruse turned into a real pain in the neck!"

"Wait! O-okay, I'll leave for today. But I'll be back to talk again tomorrow!"

"No! Don't come back at all! *Bin*—"

"Th-that's all for today! See ya!"

Chris opened the window and leaped out, nearly in tears. She disappeared into town. Dawn was just breaking.

Arrrgh. Seriously, no more dangerous stuff! Tell me again what happened to my supposed good luck.

O goddess of good fortune, Honored Eris—I'll even convert to the Eris Church when we get back to Axel. Just please let me live in peace!

With that prayer, I settled back into bed…

…until I was woken up again by a blaring announcement that might as well have been aimed directly at me.

Chapter 4

May There Be Bad Influences for This Sheltered Princess!

1

"Demon King army attack warning! Demon King army attack warning! A group presumed to be from the Demon King's army has been sighted in the field near the capital! Knights, prepare to sortie. The enemy group appears to be quite large this time, so we ask that all adventurers in the capital participate in the battle! All high-level adventurers, please assemble in front of the castle immediately!"

The announcement rang through the streets of the capital as dawn broke. At the same moment, our once-quiet inn was filled with a ruckus.

Darkness pounded on my door in a panic. "Kazuma, are you awake?! Did you hear that?! Get your stuff ready!"

"I'm asleep."

"Moron, this is no time to joke around! The Demon King's army is here—we have to get out there and help!"

I let only my head emerge from my blankets as the pounding continued. "You're the one who's joking! Did you hear that announcement? They want 'high-level' adventurers. I'm only Level 17—barely mid-level! They've got Mitsurugi and lots of other perfectly good adventurers, I'm sure. They'll be fine without us."

"Y-you impossible man! Fine! Aqua and Megumin and I are going! *Low*-level adventurers can just stay in bed and hide!" The knocking on my door turned to footsteps retreating quickly down the hall.

Finally, some peace and quiet...

"Noooo! Why do I have to go to something that dangerous?! I came to the capital to have fun! And now you want me to fight the Demon King's army? No thank you!"

"Aqua, now is no time to be thinking of yourself! You can never have too many healers in a battle with the Demon King! And look at Megumin! Look how excited she is to get out there..."

"Darkness, I will not go to the castle but shall go directly to where the Demon King's army awaits! For once the battle starts and our forces get close to those of the Demon King, I can't use my magic! I was made for the vanguard! In fact, my powered-up magic might just finish them all in one fell swoop!"

"Wait, Megumin, don't do anything reckless! And Aqua, will you let go of your bed already?! Arrrgh! Kazuma, I'm begging you, do something!"

Aren't they ever going to shut up?!

Anyway, when I got back to Axel, my money worries would be over. *Why should I stick my neck out and take part in a battle where I have nothing to—?*

"?!"

I kicked off my covers and jumped up.

The reward I might get for participating in this battle held no attraction for me. But if I could look good, make people see that I'd accomplished something... Yes! It would cancel out my failure to catch the "righteous thief"!

Not to mention, it seemed like there were plenty of "cheaters" here in the capital, not the least Mitsurugi. It didn't seem possible for us to lose, and meanwhile, I would have an opportunity to strut my stuff, protect the castle, and then maybe get my chance to hang out there again.

I didn't have to personally defeat the whole army or anything. I just had to get noticed.

"Stop it, Darkness—I've got a bad feeling about this! Goddess's intuition! Just like that time I dropped my ice cream right after I bought it or when I checked all those lottery tickets outside that store and they were all losers! Something's going to happen—I just know it! So please, let's not do this today! I'll even give you one of my sausage links at breakfast!"

"Darkness, let go of me! I am carving my legend! 'When the king's forces arrived at the battlefield, all they saw were the smoldering remains of the Demon King's army and a single wizard calmly leaving the scene of the carnage…' This is my chance! You have to let me go!"

"Kazuma! I can't do it alone—help me out with these two!"

I opened the door, completely dressed for battle, to find the three of them fighting.

"What are you doing? The kingdom is in crisis. Now come on, let's go! They need us!"

"""""   """""
......

When we showed up in front of the castle, we found the place crowded with knights clad in full sets of pristine armor, as well as tons of adventurers.

Someone I assumed was an employee of the local guild was speaking through a megaphone-like magical item. "All adventurers, gather over here, please! We have no special instructions for you. You haven't been trained to work as a group, so we won't try to have you coordinate with the knight units. Please fight on your own initiative! We'll check your Adventurer's Cards before the battle. Afterward, based on the number of monsters you defeat, you will receive a reward—so give it your all!"

We assembled where she had indicated, and another employee asked us to give her our Adventurer's Cards. When she saw my card, her brow furrowed, and she said apologetically, "Mr. Kazuma Satou, is that right? I'm sorry, but anyone below Level 30 who isn't an advanced class is going to be in danger, and we cannot allow them to participate in the battle. If I could ask you to stay here and help fortify the town…"

"It's all right. That man is a very capable adventurer with quite a history."

It was Claire. When had she gotten there? In fact, quite a few nobles had shown up in front of the castle, maybe to help encourage us adventurers or the knights.

As the nobles looked at me, I couldn't help feeling they all had great expectations. I may have failed at catching the thief, but they knew I had defeated several generals of the Demon King and wanted to see me in action.

Then a figure appeared on the castle balcony, watching us from above. When I looked closely, I realized she was focused on me, her eyes shining with hope. It was Iris.

Well, now the tension was ratcheting up.

Leave it to me! Just watch your big bro work!

At that moment, I felt a tugging on my sleeve.

"Kazuma, Kazuma! I'm smart! I *can* learn! And I definitely think I'm going to get in trouble if we participate in this battle. Like, some crazy kid will blow me up in her explosion or some muscle-headed noblewoman is going to bring a bunch of monsters my way. It's not too late—we can still go home to Axel. Let's go home, okay?"

"Aqua is not the only one who is capable of learning from the past. I will not make the same mistake twice—no one is getting caught up in any of my explosions!"

"H-hey, Aqua, you think you could stop calling me muscle-headed? People are going to start thinking I'm the least intelligent of the four of us…"

I met Aqua's anxiety with an uncharacteristic smile. "Aw, what? We're just facing a bunch of small fry who have nothing but their numbers to rely on. Just wait—you're finally gonna see me get really serious!"

""""Ooooh!"""""

My declaration made the nobles even more excited.

Then Claire shouted an order to the assembled knights and adventurers:

"All forces gathered to repel the Demon King's army—move out!"

2

"…Oh, hi. I haven't seen you in a while, Lady Eris."

"……………………"

Quicker than you could blink, I was standing in that familiar sanctuary.

How many times had I died now? There was the time General Winter offed me and that time I fell out of a tree. And now…

"I'm sorry. At my level, I didn't think there was any way some kobolds could do me in…"

A pack of kobolds had made me their punching bag.

Kobolds! Yes, *those* kobolds. Nice, easy prey—practically shrimps even in this world. And they'd killed me.

I turned to Eris, who still hadn't said a word.

"It's not what you think, milady! It was going great at first. I had Aqua's buffs, and I was sticking close to Darkness. Since the other adventurers had already dealt with the really nasty monsters, I thought I could at least beat them on numbers."

"……………………"

Yeah… It had all been going great for a while.

I kept practically in Darkness's shadow, firing arrows from relative safety, racking up one victory after another. The battle got to where the two armies were really clashing. A kobold had bitten Aqua, and she was crying up a storm, so I went and saved her…

"That kobold was no match for me. I started thinking, *Hey, even I've improved a little*, so I started chasing him…"

He'd looked really weak. So I was hot on his heels, but then all of a sudden, I realized I was surrounded by kobolds, and they promptly took their revenge.

Now what was I going to do? It would be really embarrassing to be brought back to life at that moment. Before the battle, I had made such a big deal of what a great job I was going to do—and then I'd been clobbered by Baby's First Monster. It was so pathetic, it wasn't even funny.

It was also starting to bother me that Eris hadn't said a word since I'd gotten there.

"Uh…um, Lady Eris? I know I died a really stupid death because I got a little full of myself, and I'm very sorry about it. Do you think you could…spare me a smile about now?" I asked hesitantly.

Eris began to blush as she said, "…Sexual harassment is *wrong*." She fixed me with a glare.

I felt sweat dribble down my back. Come to think of it, Eris could see what was happening on the mortal plane, couldn't she? She had to be angry that I had turned one of her precious followers into my plaything.

"No, milady, hear me out! I didn't have any choice! When I first grabbed her, her chest was so flat, I thought she was a man, and… No! I'm sorry; forgive me! I won't make any more excuses!"

I threw myself at her feet in complete submission. I could sense her mood worsening by the moment.

"…Gracious. You really do resort to sexual harassment way too much. I'll forgive you, but just this once." She sighed and scratched her cheek as if she was embarrassed.

"Thank you, Lady Eris! Ah, I don't know what I'd do if a righteous heroine–type like you started to hate me!"

"I think you might be getting carried away again… Aren't you satisfied with the little sister you've gained recently?"

Just how much have you seen from up here, Lady Eris?

I didn't quite know what to say, but Eris giggled.

"I guess that's enough teasing you for today. Anyway, there's something I'd like to ask you to do."

"…Something *you* want *me* to do?"

She nodded. "I think my follower whom you were groping last night gave you most of the details. Some of the Sacred Treasures my senior, Aqua, handed out are no longer with their original owners."

"Oh yeah, I guess she did mention something like that. But I thought Sacred Treasures chose their owners. I got an enchanted sword as a 'cheat item' once, but it turned out that if anyone but its owner used it, it was just a normal sword."

That's right: When I'd taken Mitsurugi's magical sword from him, I had thought about using it myself, but I had quickly been informed that it didn't work that way.

"That's true to an extent, but... Well, it's accurate to say that the full powers of most magical items only activate for those to whom they were originally given. An enchanted sword that can cut through anything becomes a regular sword. A special staff that allows unlimited MP turns into a normal staff. In those cases, even if someone tried to use the item for evil, it wouldn't be that big a deal."

Eris went on to explain, however, that the two Sacred Treasures that had gone missing were capable of causing an awful lot of trouble even without their full powers.

First there was the Treasure that allowed the user to summon a monster and control it with no price or penalty. In someone else's hands, it could still summon a random monster; it was just that a price would be required.

As for the Treasure that let the user change bodies with someone else, it too could still be used, but the switch would be for only a limited time; it couldn't be maintained forever.

Apparently, both these items required you to say a special phrase to activate them, so even if someone else got hold of them, it wouldn't necessarily be easy to use them.

But there was such a thing as sheer dumb chance. If someone just happened to say the correct phrase, a whole town might suddenly be full of monsters, and then there'd be trouble. Or say someone was out walking their dog and got body-switched by bad luck; we could be dealing with a whole new type of kobold.

"If we can get the items back and give them to Aqua, she'll seal them up," Eris said. "There's no reward for doing this job, and you won't gain honor or glory. Nor can you tell anyone except those you trust most about the Sacred Treasures. Even if their power is greatly reduced outside their owners' hands, someone besides one of our transplants might think of something nasty to do with them."

She took my hands, a serious expression on her face.

"Please, will you get the Sacred Treasures back?"

3

When I opened my eyes, I saw Aqua giving me a wide smile.

"Welcome back, Kazuma! Those kobolds sure did a number on you!"

I really wanna smack her!

"Is that the first thing you think to say to someone who just came back to life?! You could learn a thing or two about proper goddess etiquette from Lady Eris!"

I looked around and realized that the battle was already over. "...Hey, I'm glad you brought me back and all, but couldn't you have done it a little sooner? Like, soon enough for me to get in on the glory?"

"You were killed by kobolds. Why would I bring you back in the middle of a battle? You'd just die again, and it'd be a big pain."

Having just been killed, I couldn't find a response.

"...Hey, I've been meaning to ask. Don't you kind of smell like alcohol? You didn't skip out on the battle so you could go drink, did you?"

"No way! It's because people bought me all kinds of drinks as offerings for being so much help in our victory. Everyone did an amazing job while you were lying there dead. My Turn Undead and healing magic were crucial—I wish you could have seen it!"

...That made sense. It explained why the looks Aqua was getting seemed unusually full of respect and reverence.

"Okay, one last thing... Why is there some kind of weight tied to me?"

"Oh, that. See, Darkness didn't want your body to accidentally get damaged during the battle, so she said to put it in a corner where it would be safe. And I did put you in a corner, but monsters kept trying to drag you away…"

"Stop right there! I don't want to hear any more! I get it; you stuck this weight to me so they wouldn't carry me off! Thank you very much! But I can't help thinking—maybe you guys could take a little more care when you handle the dead!"

Now that I had a sense of what had happened, I took another look around. This time, the Demon King's attack had been on a pretty major scale. I was too inexperienced to guess the number at a glance, but I estimated there were well over a thousand monster corpses there. And yet, on our side, I didn't see anyone who even looked wounded, let alone dead.

That was when several knights came up to us, full of thanks.

"Miss Aqua, you've done an amazing job reviving the dead! Now, please, this way!"

"Whoo! That's some Arch-priest! What talent! To think she can even use Resurrection!"

"It's all thanks to her that there are no wounded left around here! Thank you so much, Miss Aqua!"

Ah, so she had healed everyone who was injured. I never would have expected it—she was usually such a ditz.

"Kazuma, you're alive! Are you all right? Everything feeling okay?"

Darkness, her face and armor covered in soot, came up with several knights in tow. To judge by all the gouges in her armor, she had worked hard.

The knights looked at her with admiring gazes, and they had nothing but good things to say.

"Lady Dustiness, your performance today was exemplary!"

"Yes, indeed! The sight of you diving into the enemy ranks, completely calm despite the magic that was being unleashed upon you—my heart trembled to see it!"

"Did you notice the look on the Demon King's commander's face when he saw her? I shan't soon forget that!"

"Lady Dustiness, your willingness to take the enemy's attacks upon yourself helped prevent many casualties. You've saved us all!"

I see. In a battle of this magnitude, Darkness's Decoy skill probably would have been a lot of help. Even if she couldn't hit the broad side of a barn, Darkness was the best defender in Axel.

I was a little disappointed I had missed the relatively unusual sight of Darkness really strutting her stuff. And come to think of it, where was Megumin?

No sooner had I thought this than I spotted her on a stretcher, being carried along as carefully as if she were a broken doll. The knights around the stretcher shooed away any curious adventurers.

"MVP of the battle coming through! Make way!"

"Miss Megumin is tired—get out of the way! You want to be wiped off the face of the earth with an explosion?"

"Make way for Miss Megumin, first among the spell-casters of Axel and she who reduces all to ash!"

...What the hell?

When I really concentrated, I could see a huge crater in the distance.

"At first, everyone was really close, so Megumin couldn't use her magic, right?" Aqua said. "But as things got worse and worse for them, the Demon King's army started to fall back. Finally, the enemy commander goes: *'This battle was just the start! One day we'll be back with a much bigger army, and we'll turn this place to ash!'* And then they tried to run away..."

"And then it was awesome! Miss Megumin planted an explosion right in the middle of the fleeing troops, all, *'My name is Megumin! First among the spell-casters of Axel and master of Explosion! It shall be you who are reduced to ash...!'* Just awesome!"

"Yeah, have you ever seen anything cooler? It's incredible how she used up her entire supply of MP just to cast that one spell for us!"

Megumin, who rode on that stretcher like she was on the shrine float at a festival, seemed more than pleased to be treated like this.

"Is that so? I see! Well, such insignificant opponents could hardly be expected to stand up to my most powerful technique! After all, my Explosion has buried more than one general of the Demon King, to say nothing of Destroyer, the legendary bounty head!"

It was incredible, all right. Incredible how much she let this go to her head while she lay on that litter.

"So it's true that Destroyer is gone?!"

"What a great and powerful wizard! Miss Megumin, could you possibly show us some of your other, non-Explosion spells?"

"Oh yeah! I want to see just how much power there is in your advanced magic!"

"...Yes, and of course, I dearly want to show you, but sadly, I've used up my MP for now. So unfortunately..."

"Of course, of course! We can wait till tomorrow, Miss Megumin!"

"Ooh, I can't wait till tomorrow morning!"

"I'm gonna tell everyone to come and see!"

"...Y-yes. But, ahem, I might be busy tomorrow... Oh, Kazuma! Thank goodness Aqua was able to bring you back to life! It must be hard for you, having just been resurrected. Why don't you let me look after you tomorrow?"

Megumin had gotten so carried away with herself that things were threatening to get out of hand. Frankly, I thought I'd like to see where it went.

4

"The knights and the adventurers are back!"

Those words—I couldn't tell who had shouted them—were the cue for the whole capital to erupt into a joyous welcome.

As we headed to the castle to debrief, the townspeople sang our praises. Some bowed deeply, while others pumped their fists in the air. It brought proud smiles to the faces of the returning heroes.

When we got to the castle, a crowd of jubilant nobles, headed up by Iris and Claire, greeted us.

Claire, in her white suit as always, stepped out in front. "Knights and adventurers! Excellent work today! Thanks to you, the capital is safe once again. Princess Iris offers you all her profound thanks on behalf of this nation. You may expect a healthy reward!"

That got a cheer from the adventurers.

"In addition! A feast is being prepared for tonight to help restore you. You must be very tired after that battle. Rest yourselves until this evening, and then come back to the castle. Those who distinguished themselves will be given special rewards! That will be all—and thank you again for your fine work!"

The cheer rose to a fever pitch, the adventurers almost wild with joy, and then they went their separate ways to decide how to pass the time until that evening.

"Lady Dustiness, please come to the castle; tell us all about what happened...!"

"Yes, I heard it was quite a frightful encounter...!"

"By all means, Lady Dustiness, regale us with your deeds!"

Darkness was immediately surrounded by nobles and shepherded off to the castle. She looked to us for help as they practically dragged her away, but as the guy who was killed by kobolds, I was feeling pretty embarrassed and didn't want to garner any attention if I could help it.

"Hey, Kazuma. I'm gonna kill time until the party starts by asking the people I healed if they want to join the Axis Church. They owe me for fixing them up, so I'm gonna go cash in!"

"I'm sure they're perfectly thankful even if you don't 'cash in.' Stunts like this are why you never get new believers."

Aqua completely ignored me, going up to the nearest knight. As I watched her, a voice came from behind me.

"Oh, you can let me down here. I'll get a piggyback ride from my party member."

It was Megumin, of course. The knights who had been ferrying her around gently set her on the ground. From there, she beckoned to me. *Does she realize I exist for more than giving her piggyback rides?*

"I just came back from the dead," I said. "I thought *you* were going to take care of *me*?"

"And so I shall, starting tomorrow. But for today, please indulge me. Kazuma, let's go back to Axel tomorrow. First thing in the morning, if possible."

I bent down and hefted Megumin onto my back; she wrapped her arms around my neck in a familiar motion. That was when Iris came up to us wearing an innocent smile.

"I'm so glad you're all right, Elder Brother! Welcome home!"

"Elder Brother?!" Megumin exclaimed.

"Oh, Iris! I wasn't all right for a while there, though. I actually died—but I came back to life."

That stopped her in her tracks, a look of amazement on her face.

"You died?! Elder Brother, are you okay?! Come into the castle and rest up until the feast—the room you were using is just the way you left it!"

" 'Elder Brother' again?!"

"Thanks. But you don't have to worry so much. I'm alive now, no problem."

Megumin, meanwhile, had been making a racket right next to my ear. For some reason, the words *Elder Brother* seemed to bother her.

"That's good… Then tell me, Elder Brother, were you able to distinguish yourself in battle enough that you'll be able to stay at the castle again?" She looked bright and cheerful and full of hope once more.

"Er, well…I mean, even the best of us get caught by surprise sometimes, right? Things didn't go so hot today…"

"Oh, I see… But I'm glad you at least came back safely! And even if you didn't do a lot of valorous deeds, you did go out and fight to defend the capital. So I'll ask Claire again if you can stay in the castle, Elder Brother!"

"…"

"Thanks, Iris. But the way I died this time was really pathetic, so I don't have much hope... Anyway, catch you tonight."

At that, Iris seemed incredibly sad.

"...It seems this Iris girl has become quite fond of you in the brief time you were away," Megumin said from my back once Iris had followed Claire into the castle.

"I know, right? I got the little sister I've always wanted. Maybe I really do like 'em young."

"...When we get back to town, should I start calling you Big Brother?"

"Nah, you're my jailbait, remember? I don't like mixing archetypes."

"You know, you can stop treating me like a jailbait character anytime now!"

Perched on my back, Megumin was in the perfect position to try to strangle me as I headed for my room.

5

We came to the room in the castle where I had stayed, and I set Megumin down on the couch. She looked around in amazement.

"My! This is quite a nice room. And you just stayed here while maids and butlers took care of you? I think I can see now why you didn't want to come home."

"Right? There was great food, and everyone babied me. If you lived here, you wouldn't want to come home, either. Ah, but I didn't manage to do anything noteworthy in the battle. I guess we'll have to go home tomorrow..."

I took off my equipment and sat on the bed, kicking my feet aimlessly.

Megumin, still tired from a lack of MP, said, "...But I think that may be for the best. As much as I've enjoyed our upscale life in the capital, I think I prefer our lives in Axel. Everyone going on quests together, our impassioned arguments… The four of us can all be together again, starting tomorrow." And she gave her most genuine smile.

"Oh! Y-yeah, you're right. I mean, I was never that serious about wanting to stay at the castle…!" I found myself strangely agitated by her reaction. I kicked my feet a little harder to cover for myself.

"Is that so? Are you not happy with that Iris girl?" Megumin said teasingly. She seemed to be enjoying this.

Excuse me? Iris was never anything more than a little sister to me.

But I'd admit, it was hard to just leave her there. She seemed so lonely—but not in quite the way that, say, Yunyun seemed lonely.

Just then…

"Elder Brother, could I have a moment…?"

…Iris's voice came through the door.

"I'm so sorry, Elder Brother. I tried to talk to Claire, but she says you just can't stay at the castle."

Iris was sitting next to Megumin, sniffling.

"It is what it is. I'm sorry I couldn't do more to prove my worth."

"You don't have to apologize, Elder Brother. You risked your life on the battlefield—in fact, you *gave* your life…" As she spoke, Iris looked at me with eyes full of tears. She seemed so serious, I couldn't bring myself to tell her that I'd been carried off by a bunch of kobolds and beaten to death. Instead, I just returned her gaze in silence.

The two of us sat there, looking at each other wordlessly.

"…Have you both forgotten that I'm here?"

"Huh?! N-no! We haven't forgotten!"

"Iris is right—we didn't forget about you, Megumin! No Lolita complexes here, so don't look at me like that! Iris is just a little sister to me; there's nothing weird between us! …W-wait, Iris, don't look so sad. People will get the wrong idea—in fact, *I* might get the wrong idea!"

Megumin ignored my admittedly suspicious behavior, suddenly seeming to notice something.

"Hmm? Now, there's a princess for you—that's quite some magical item you have. I sense far more magical power from it than you might expect. That necklace of yours—is it possible it's on the level of a Sacred Treasure? It doesn't look like anything made by the Crimson Magic Village. Where in the world did you get it?"

I guess she was interested in the necklace Iris was wearing. It was of a simple design very different from those of her other accessories.

"Oh, this? This necklace was given to my real elder brother. But since he's away on campaign, I have it right now, as the representative of the royal family."

Megumin leaned in, her eyes shining. "Yes? And what power does that magical item have? It must be something impressive—that item is far more magical than average! It must be strong enough that it could potentially destroy the world!"

Look, not everyone shares your interests...

"No, I don't think... Actually, we haven't figured out exactly how to use this item yet. We believe perhaps you have to intone a specific word or phrase in order to activate it. It's engraved with some characters that we think may represent that word, but all the king's scholars couldn't decode them..."

She turned the necklace so we could see the back. Some letters were indeed carved there...

"Huh? It's just Japanese. 'What's yours is mine, what's mine is yours. I become you!' That's really dumb. Who came up with this incantation?"

It was such a random phrase. I had serious doubts about the sanity of whoever had given this divine item to some Japanese person.

"Wha...? W-wait! Kazuma—the princess's necklace is shining!"

"E-Elder Brother?! I think you may have activated it...!"

"Huh? Wh-whoa, get rid of it! Iris, take that thing off and throw it out the window!"

I tried to pull the necklace off her neck, but the shining gem in the middle of it shot out a beam of light—!

"Huh? Nothing happened..."

I realized I had squeezed my eyes shut. When I heard Megumin's voice, I opened them again.

And I was standing in front of me.

I was reaching out toward me with shock written all over my face.

"How long do you two plan to stand there staring at each other? Please don't forget I'm here *again*." She sighed in exasperation, apparently ignoring the bizarre circumstances.

"Cram it, Megumin, something really weird is going on here!"

"My goodness, Your Highness, are we suddenly on a first-name basis? I'm older than you, so if you're comfortable addressing Kazuma as Elder Brother, you can call me 'Big Sis Megumin' or 'Elder Sister.' For that matter, I really don't think you should talk that way. Claire or whoever she is said she thought Kazuma was a bad influence on you, but it sounds like it's too late now."

For some reason, Megumin was eyeing me like I was a naughty child.

Then the me I was looking at waved my hands frantically. "Uh, um... Excuse me, but *I'm* Iris..."

Everyone in the room went dead silent.

"W-w-w-w-w-wait, *I'm* Iris now?! You mean this is—! Ahhhh! It's really truuuuue! I'm in a dress! I'm in a frilly dress! What is this strange new feeling?! It's like I've woken up to find out someone put women's clothes on me!"

"Elder Brother?! You're in my body?! Please don't do that; it's shameful!"

"Hang on, Iris; I see all sorts of problems here! This skirt is a disaster waiting to happen. I've got no confidence about my lower body! This is incredible—do women really walk around in public so defenseless?!"

I held up the hem of the dress, but I—or rather, Iris in my body—clung to me, nearly weeping.

"Elder Brother, no more! Please stop there!"

"Stop?! I think I know what's happening here, but with my skirt up and me—I mean you—I mean Kazuma—grabbing me like that, what are people going to think?!"

At that moment, there was a knock on the door.

"Your Highness?! I hear screaming—is something wrong?!"

It was Claire. She must have been just outside as Iris's bodyguard.

I plastered myself against the door so it wouldn't open.

"C-Claire? It, um, it is nothing! Indeed, I was merely conversing with Elder Brother, and we became rather excited!"

"A-are you sure? That's all right, then, but don't spend too long talking with that man. He speaks nothing but rubbish."

"I'm fine…! You may go back to…bodyguarding now!"

Wearing a dress and trying my best to talk like a princess, I was experiencing something entirely new. I leaned against the door and slid to the ground.

The three of us sat in a circle in the middle of the room, trying to decide what to do about these bodies.

"Now what do we do?" I said. "I'm not exactly averse to living the rest of my life as a beautiful, pampered girl, but I admit it's hard to let go of the body I've spent my entire life in. How can we get back to normal?"

"I'm not sure, but I think you just nonchalantly said something incredible," Megumin said. "Tell me, how are you two? No pain? Not feeling ill?"

"No, I seem to be fine. If anything… Well, I feel big and powerful in a man's body. I'd sort of like to go on an adventure."

"I'm sorry, Your Highness, but maybe you could speak just a little less politely with that mouth." Megumin looked like she might cry.

"Well, this is trouble. We tried the activation phrase again, but the necklace just glowed. So we can't swap right back, and that's bad," I said.

It was true; we had tried to use the necklace's power again, but we hadn't switched back.

"Perhaps there's a different phrase that undoes the spell," Megumin said. "This is some item, though. The power to switch bodies! I've never heard of such a potent artifact."

Iris sniffed as she spoke. "What are we going to do? What if we can never go back to normal? I have to live out the rest of my life as an adventurer...? Forced out of the castle, living a wild and free life of adventure... Finding trustworthy companions, destroying one evil monster after another, traveling to places I've never seen...! Elder Brother, what am I going to do?! I'm not sure I would be completely unhappy if we can't go back to normal!" She had gone from sniffling to somewhat pleased.

"Princess, please calm down! What you're saying is foolishness!" Megumin cried.

True, we really couldn't go on like this. If the magic item's power was some form of curse, we might be able to ask Aqua to do something about it...

Thinking of Aqua reminded me: She was the one who had given this body-swap item to some Japanese person to begin with...!

"It's okay! I know what this item is! It's a particular Sacred Treasure. If anyone besides the original owner uses it, the switch only lasts for a limited time. I don't know exactly how long, but it means we won't be stuck like this forever."

That brought a sigh of relief from Megumin. Iris, though, seemed strangely conflicted.

"So all we have to do is wait, and we'll go back to normal. Sure hope it happens before the party tonight..." I tossed myself onto the bed, intending to sleep until then.

"E-Elder Brother! I want... I have a request!" Iris was seated formally on the floor, her legs folded neatly beneath her and her face serious. Seeing myself in that position, I couldn't help thinking I was being bullied. I wished she would sit less formally.

"You have a— Ahaaa, I get it. You're getting to be that age, aren't you? Wondering about a guy's body? Sorry, but keep your hands off!"

"I—I was thinking no such thing! What about you, Elder Brother? Can I trust you to leave my body alone?! What I want is... Just once, I'd like to try leaving the castle without any guards or servants."

She looked at me doubtfully, almost fearfully, like a child afraid of being scolded. Retainers had surrounded her from the moment she was born. She'd grown up in the capital, but I'd be willing to bet she'd never really seen the place. Even when she did get to go out, it was probably tough to enjoy looking around stores and such when you were trailed by a bunch of bodyguards.

Now, with my body, she could easily leave. But Iris totally lacked anything in the way of street smarts. Could I really let her go out alone?

As I tried to come up with an answer, Megumin, who at that point hadn't said anything, let out a sigh. "Very well. I can see there's no choice. You can't go with her, Kazuma, in that body. I will accompany her. Don't worry, I won't harangue you like your retainers. I will just watch out for you in case you get into any fights."

"Cut it out! What the hell good are you gonna do?!"

But Iris, smiling broadly, stood up. "Okay then, let's go, Elder Sister!"

"...Erm, I know I told you to call me that earlier, but I think you'd better stick to 'Megumin'..."

Are these two really going to be okay?

"A pleasure, Miss Megumin!"

"You can count on me. I shall teach you many things, from how to haggle when shopping to how to accept a fight when someone throws down the gauntlet."

Argh, they'll be fine, won't they?!

6

Once Iris and Megumin were on their way, I wandered around the castle with Claire in tow. Since "I" had left, it would be strange for the princess to remain in my room. I just figured I would kill time until Iris had had her fill of the outside world and came back.

But as I walked around with my head held high, I noticed that everyone was bowing to me. I nodded magnanimously at each of them.

Uh-oh. This is kind of nice. I could get used to this.

"Your Highness, did anything happen in that man's room? Ever since you came out of there, you've seemed… Well, let's just say I'm starting to wonder if he was telling you inappropriate stories again." Claire piped up from behind me with insults at the ready.

"Claire, you mustn't say such things about Master Kazuma. He is a most wonderful person. I don't think it would be wrong for his name to go down in our nation's history textbooks."

"Now I really *do* wonder what he said to you, Your Highness! I think it's about time we got rid of him…"

I wish she wouldn't say things like that when she's right behind me.

As we wandered the castle, we saw adventurers here and there. They must have been passing the time until the victory party that night. A careful look revealed a group who had done an especially good job during the battle. Judging by how many of them had black hair and black eyes, they were probably Japanese like me. It was definitely tempting to talk to them—they were from my own country—but it wouldn't have been very easy to do in this body.

"Well, if it isn't Princess Iris and Miss Claire."

I recognized that voice. Claire smiled when she saw its owner.

"Ah, Master Mitsurugi. I hear you acquitted yourself brilliantly, as usual! I must apologize that you always seem to end up right in the heart of danger."

The adventurer who had called out to us was none other than Mitsurugi. He was giving us his most handsome smile.

"Not at all. I would hardly even call that danger. And anyway, it's my duty to protect the princess and the people of this country." Then he gave me a friendly pat on the head.

"Claire, this man is touching my head far too casually. Execute him immediately."

"What?!"

"Your Highness, you truly have been acting strange. What in the world is going on?!"

I guess Mitsurugi must have been so used to patting girls' heads and smiling at them that he just did it unconsciously now. I shooed him away and resumed my exploration of the castle.

There was a reason for all my snooping around.

"Say, Claire, where's Lalatina? I want to tease—I mean, I want to congratulate her on her fine work in today's battle."

"Lady Dustiness was hit by some fire magic during the battle and covered in ashes, so right now she's in the bath."

"Claire! Take me to her immediately! I shall join her and wash her back!"

"Your Highness?! What in the world has happened to you? Even with Lady Dustiness's station, for a royal to wash a retainer's back…"

"Perhaps I shall wash yours, too, Claire, to thank you for your tireless service. Are you opposed?"

"No objections from me, Your Highness! Let's go—let's go right now!"

Claire, who had always shown a slightly strange level of loyalty toward Iris, went off in excitement, the expression on her face a bit dangerous.

When we got to the changing room of the castle baths, we ran into Darkness, apparently just out of the tub. Sadly, she was already done changing.

"Oh, Your Highness," she said. "Planning to wash up before the party?" She smiled at me, drying her hair with a towel.

"No, Lalatina—I wanted to wash your back, since you did such a great job in the battle today… But it looks like I'm too late. What a shame…"

I looked disappointedly at the ground as I spoke. That sent Darkness into a bit of a panic. "N-not at all! Far be it from me to let your kind offer be in vain! We still have time—I can take another bath!" Then she hurriedly began stripping off her clothes.

"Dark—! I mean, L-Lalatina! Slow down—don't just rip off your clothes like that without any hint of embarrassment! I wasn't ready!"

"Y-Your Highness, what's going on? Your face is awfully red..." Darkness, half-undressed, was looking at me with concern.

She was right next to me, and I could see her underwear... *Hang on—I don't think she's wearing a bra!*

Oh, she'd be wearing a dress for the party, and her bra line would show!

As I stood there staring dumbly at Darkness, Claire came up wearing nothing but a towel and a worried expression. "Your Highness, do you have a fever? Come to think of it, you haven't been looking yourself..."

Then she put her long, delicate hands on my cheeks...!

Now, at last, I understood.

I got why the Japanese guy who had come here before me had asked for this Sacred Treasure.

True, when we went back to normal, Iris might figure out by the scent of soap that I had been in the bath. But at this point, I was definitely not thinking that far ahead. One of my illustrious Japanese forebears had left us these words: Worry about tomorrow...tomorrow.

O Eris, goddess of good fortune. I have never been so thankful for my amazing Luck.

I offered up this prayer as I stood with a gorgeous, half-naked woman on either side of me. Then I reached to start taking off my own clothes...

...and felt my consciousness growing dim.

"—'s just perfect! If you think you can say stuff like that to my older brother, I guess you know what you're getting yourself into!"

"Th-this bastard! Did you hear what he said about our brother?! Look! You made him cry!"

"H-hey, shut up, idiot, I ain't cryin'! I just got a little surprised 'cause no one's ever talked to me like that before!"

I was staring down three very angry-looking men.

…Lady Eris, this kind of bait and switch is really too much.

7

"Well said, that's the way! Now put the final nail in the coffin! Say, *I'm done talking. And I don't have time to waste—I'm gonna turn you guys into experience points!* If you can say that, you pass! Then all that's left is to reduce these guys to quivering heaps!"

Megumin was shouting enthusiastically from my back.

Hang on a second. What's going on here?

I mean, I'd obviously gone back to normal, but I was also about to get in a fight—what were Megumin and Iris up to?!

"Make fun'a me, will you? I'll show you!"

The guy right in front of me—the one the others had called their older brother—launched himself at me with a flying punch and tears in his eyes, even though I had no idea what I'd said to him.

"Gah! H-hey, jerk! No fair! Can't you see I'm carrying someone right now?! If we're gonna go at it, at least let me set her down first!"

"No fair?! You were the one who said, 'I don't even need to get serious against wimps like you. I'll take on all three of you at once, and I'll leave this girl here as a handicap'!"

"When are you gonna get tired of being mean to our bro?! What'd he ever do to you?!"

"I don't even care anymore; let's get this guy! Treat us like common street thugs, will he? We'll show him!"

Apparently, I'd managed to only tick them off even more.

"Kazuma, I see you're back to normal! Give me some MP with Drain Touch so I can take part in this battle, too!"

"You deliberately got us into this, didn't you?! *You* do something about it!"

Teary-eyed and rubbing the cheek where the guy's punch had landed, I poured my MP into Megumin...

"...They really were just small fry. I can't blame them, in the face of my overwhelming power."

"You might be a wizard, but you're also a high-level adventurer. You shouldn't go after ordinary people like that!"

We had triumphed in the one-on-three battle, but we had also attracted a lot of unwanted attention, so we hurried back to the castle.

"I really wanted to give the princess a chance to shine, but you came back at just the right moment. I'm a little sorry she couldn't be here."

"Look, what did you plan to do if anything had happened to Iris? Getting that delicate princess in a fight? What were you thinking?"

Megumin looked puzzled. "I think the question, Kazuma, is what are *you* thinking? Members of the royal family are quite powerful. In addition to their natural talents, they learn how to fight from a young age in order to protect themselves. To be blunt, that princess is stronger than you. Even in your body, she likely wouldn't have had any trouble winning."

What, seriously?

"Okay, but how did you even get into that fight? Those guys looked like bad news; what did you do to them?"

"The princess and I went to a number of different shops before we ran into that lot on a deserted street."

I see. And it went from there...

"Normally, when such men see a girl like me, they call out something like, *Nice friend you got there. Just leave her with us—we'll take good care of her!* Right? But these guys glanced at me once, and that was it. They didn't even catcall me! So I accused them of being spineless wusses."

"You sound like some petty gangster picking a fight with innocent bystanders!"

N-now what? Maybe I should go back and apologize…

"I admit I taunted them, but they were the ones who made the first move. It's all right; if it comes to a trial, we can win. It's their fault for getting physical just because I mocked them a little."

"This from the girl who can't hold her temper over so much as a lame joke! Ugh, if we see them again, I'll have to apologize…"

As I fretted, we arrived back at the castle.

"Well, we may have gotten ourselves into some trouble, but the princess enjoyed herself very much. She got to try street food for the first time, and that made her quite happy."

"Hrm… Well, that's good, at least. Or is it? I'll bet everyone will think I'm being a bad influence on her again…"

"You have such a soft spot for that girl, Kazuma. Although I'm a little anxious when I notice how close her characteristics are to mine—for example, the fact that we are both younger than you."

"Y-you think you have anything in common with that demure, refined beauty?"

As we argued, we passed through the castle gate.

And found Darkness and Claire with their arms crossed, standing in our path.

8

I was huddled in an out-of-the-way corner of the party hall. Aqua came up to me, clutching an expensive-looking bottle of wine.

"Oh, Kazuma. How could you be so stupid? I know you usually treat me like the idiot, but today it's my turn. You're the biggest idiot in the history of idiocy!"

There was nothing I could say to the moron with the wine bottle.

Except: "It's not what you think. It's not like I meant for any of that to happen. It's just… Walking around the castle with everyone bowing to me—I started to feel like people would forgive and forget no matter what I did!"

"Once again: idiot. If you did an Internet search for the word *idiot*, your name would be the first hit!"

I wanted to grab the wine bottle she was holding and send her into a crying fit, but I could hardly speak.

The moment I had gone back to my real body, Iris, of course, had found herself in the changing room. Darkness and Claire noticed the shift in Iris's personality immediately, and when they asked her what was going on...

"I can't believe they got so mad at Iris, even. Gaaah! I'm supposed to be her big brother! I don't deserve to live..."

"...*Sigh*. Just lie low here. I'll bring you something tasty." Aqua's sudden display of kindness helped heal my delicate heart. When push came to shove, I guess she was a goddess. You could count on her when you were really feeling down...

When Megumin found out what I had been up to just before returning to my real body, she joined Darkness in ignoring my excuses.

"There's something to be said for the person who's known you the longest. I wish the others would learn from your generosity. Hey, I've been wondering, what's that wine you're holding? Come to think of it, when we went out yesterday, I remember you were looking for something good to drink. Found a souvenir?"

"Oh, this? The people from the castle said they wanted to give us a special reward for our excellent work in the battle, but when they asked what we wanted, everyone else seemed busy, so on behalf of the party, I asked for this wine."

What?! She just decided on our reward without asking us?

Anyway, let Aqua hold a bottle of wine long enough, and she was likely to drop it. I reached to take it from her so I could hold on to it until we got home.

"Well, what's done is done. Once we get back to Axel, we can all—"

—*drink it together*, I was going to say, but Aqua swatted my hand away.

"What do you think you're doing?" I said. "You're just going to fall on it or forget it somewhere, and that'll mean wasting this classy wine. If you'd bought it yourself, I wouldn't care, but this is supposed to be a reward for all of us. Come on, I'll hold it for you. Give it here."

"No way. They gave it to me, and I'm not handing it over to anyone. The person who delivered it even said, 'Oh, you all did such fine work, but you were the most amazing out of everyone, Lady Aqua!' She was thrilled nobody died in this battle, and that was because of me! I'm entitled to this as a reward."

"I don't think so! We're all responsible for the positive outcome. Anyway, that stuff looks expensive. Let me have a— Hey, come back here!"

Aqua fled so no one else could get their hands on her precious wine. And so I was by myself again…

The banquet hall was filled with little clusters of people, mostly surrounding some successful adventurer or other. The nobles, keeping their distance from the rest of the crowd, were nonetheless excited to discuss the battle.

"Heavens, what an easy victory this was! It made all the difference that Lady Dustiness's party led the charge so astutely!"

"Quite right. Lady Dustiness soaked up the foe's attacks, while Lady Aqua purified masses of undead and healed everyone's wounds in the blink of an eye. And then there was Lady Megumin, who struck the final blow to the retreating enemy! It almost seems those three alone could bring down the Demon King!"

"Indeed it does! It does seem that such a trio could go toe-to-toe with the Demon King! You know, I've heard that those three have dispatched several generals of the Demon King already. I can't say I'm surprised…"

"And let's not forget Master Mitsurugi, wielder of the enchanted blade and pride of the kingdom! If he were to join those other three, surely their party could topple the Demon King. And I think his party already has an archer girl and a spear girl in it. How perfectly balanced their group would be."

""""""That's perfect!"""""" the other nobles agreed.

Ahem—I think you're forgetting someone in all this talk of the perfect party.

I mean, I understood. I'd been killed by kobolds, after all, and was totally unable to contribute at all this time. The looks I was getting...

"So *that's* the guy who..."

"Yeah, that's him. The one Claire mentioned. All talk..."

"You know, I heard he's an Adventurer—the weakest class—and his level isn't even that high."

"I can't imagine why Lady Dustiness keeps him around."

"I hear he's pretty good at getting people to like him. He's even in Princess Iris's good favor and is planning to move into the castle..."

The constant whispering was starting to get to me—but there was some truth in it, so I couldn't even complain!

In stark contrast to me, all by my lonesome in a corner, everyone else was surrounded by both nobles and other adventurers praising them to the skies.

Megumin had a crowd of what I presumed were wizards around her. As for Aqua, all the people she had healed were mobbing her. Mitsurugi must have been used to getting along in the capital, because he greeted everyone who came up to him with practiced ease. There seemed to be a high percentage of women in his crowd.

A closer look showed that Megumin appeared to be letting the adulation go to her head, while Aqua, for some reason, was still clutching the wine close and shooing away everyone who got near her. She must've been under the impression that they were out to steal her alcohol.

And then there was...

"Heh, whatever she says, she's really the daughter of a major noble family."

Darkness was in a dress, but unlike at the party the other day, regular adventurers were participating in the victory celebration, too. Maybe that was why she was sharing a special table with the royalty and some of the high-ranking nobles. People who were probably members of the royal guard surrounded the table. I didn't think I had a shot at getting close.

I guess it was a little late, but I suddenly realized how big the social gap between us was, and it left me feeling kind of lonely.

Then I made eye contact with Iris, who was also seated at Darkness's table. She had been really angry earlier, but when she looked at me now, I thought she seemed almost sad.

I would be going home the next day. I wished the last thing I'd seen of Iris hadn't been her in a rage. If only I could have seen her smile…

At that moment, as I stood there feeling sorry for myself, somebody spoke to me. "What, you're still here at the castle?"

Even though this was a special party, the speaker was wearing her white suit as usual. Claire had a glass in one hand and was glaring daggers at me.

It wasn't enough that I had been absolutely no help in the recent battle. There had been the whole body-swapping fiasco earlier, too. Suffice it to say, she wasn't speaking to me as deferentially as she had when we'd first met.

Maybe I was having a bad influence on her, too?

"We've asked Lady Dustiness and the others to stay here tonight as guests of honor, but you can show yourself out."

"…Look, I get that you're angry with me. Even I think I went a little far this time. But it's my last night here. You think you could have a heart just this once? I mean, you seemed at least a little bit happy to get a bath with Iris."

"D-don't be stupid. What are you saying? Me, happy about a bath with the princess? That's… That's the stupidest… But never mind that. We won't speak of it."

She definitely felt something more than loyalty for Iris. Darkness and her perversions, Alderp and his creepy-old-guy mentality—were all nobles this way?

"You didn't catch the thief, and you didn't do one bit of good in the battle. You really are all talk, aren't you? I asked around, and it turns out when you defeated the Demon King's generals, you didn't even do it yourself. It was always Lady Dustiness or that wizard who struck the final blow."

This conversation was going south in a hurry.

"I was supervising them! And hey, they're not perfect, either, all right?"

"I'm already familiar with their shortcomings. But it's nothing that can't be compensated for with some backup from our nation. I presume they'll be asked to join Mitsurugi's party. Together, I suspect they could defeat even the Demon King. You have more than enough money already, don't you? Maybe you could just leave that party and spend the rest of your life lolling around town."

Wait a second, what's this all of a sudden?

"I'm all for lolling around, but where do you get off trying to force me out of my own party? I knew a young punk who thought a lot like you, but I had him join up with Aqua and the others, and he went home crying. You want to try corralling that lot?"

"They only need to work as part of a group, as they did today. Each of them has one very specific focus, but with a large enough group, that's fine. And what about you? Do you excel in any one thing, the way they do? Well, think about it. If you can show some ability that puts those girls and Mitsurugi to shame, then you can feel free to laugh at me to your heart's content."

Asking me to show what I was capable of the very same day I got killed by kobolds. *What a sadist! Fine. Forget this castle! I'm going back to my inn.*

…Wait, that's right.

"Let's forget all that for a minute. What about the necklace Iris was wearing? Where did it go? Don't let her keep it. I think it's some kind of Sacred Treasure. If you give it to my friend Aqua, she'll seal it away. Could you do that for me?"

Claire's response to this warning surprised me.

"I can't do that. That necklace was a gift to His Highness, the first prince, Jatice. As His Highness hasn't returned yet, it's not mine to give away. Anyway, it may be a Sacred Treasure, but all it does is let you switch bodies for a while. Where's the harm in that?"

She blushed a little, looking off to one side.

…She was actually encouraged by all that fuss today.

Maybe it didn't matter. If you didn't invoke the activation phrase, it was just a necklace. And you really didn't switch bodies for very long.

Then Claire gave me a thin smile and said, "I want you out of the capital tomorrow. We don't need your strength or your abilities. If you refuse to go, I'll evict you by force… But anyway, feel free to celebrate tonight… That is, if you've done anything worth celebrating."

9

I went back to our inn with tears in my eyes and sat alone in my dark room, sobbing.

"This sucks! What's her problem anyway? We won't see each other again after tomorrow, and she still can't bring herself to say one nice thing to me? I mean, I know it's partly my fault! In fact, it's all my fault!"

Darkness and the others had made no attempt to extricate themselves from their admirers, so I assumed they were going to stay until the end of the party and sleep at the castle.

…They wouldn't really go to Mitsurugi's party, would they?

Why did this feel so wrong? All along, I'd wanted nothing more than to ditch those deadweights and join a real party, but now that it might actually happen—for some reason, I was really anxious…

Arrrgh, forget it! I'll just go back to Axel and live a life of leisure on the reward money from Sylvia and the payment from Vanir.

I wondered what I'd do first when I got back to town. I was all for a life of leisure, but even I might get tired of just sleeping all day, every day. It really sucked that this world didn't have video games or PCs.

But wait—there was that game system Aqua brought back from Crimson Magic Village. Perfect! I'd just get it from her and spend my days playing games to my heart's content.

As this fantasy was running through my mind, I realized something.

I never got to show Iris who's boss at our game...

So I sat around, thinking of Iris and moping. That was when it happened: There was a knock at the window of my room.

I looked out. In the moonlight, I could discern the silver-haired thief girl perched on my window frame two stories up.

I opened the window, and Chris slipped into the room.

"Heyo. Didn't you have a party today? Left early?" Then she laughed as if she knew exactly what had happened, which she probably did. How *did* she know about the Sacred Treasures and what had gone on at the party anyway? I wondered if there was some kind of "thieves guild" that only thieves could belong to.

"Sneak into my room at night as many times as you want, but my answer's not going to change. However, I will share some info with you that I happened to pick up. The Sacred Treasure that allows people to change bodies is in the castle. But you really only get to switch for a very short time. It doesn't seem that dangerous, not like the monster-summoning one."

I turned toward her just long enough to say all this, then rolled over again in my bed, my back to her. Tonight of all nights, I wanted to be left to my memories of Iris. I knew Lady Eris had asked me to handle the Sacred Treasures when she brought me back from the dead, but right at that moment, I couldn't muster the motivation.

Chris spoke to my back. "With that item, if one of you dies during the switch, the other one can't go back to normal," she nonchalantly explained, even though I couldn't care le—

"...Wait. What did you just say?" I sat up.

Chris smirked at my panicked expression. "It's actually an extremely powerful magical item. If you use it right, you could even gain eternal life with it. When your body gets weak, just swap with a young, healthy person and kill the old body. If you transfer your assets before you make the switch, even better."

Okay, this was no laughing matter. I could see what made this a Sacred Treasure. But right now, Chris and I were the only people who knew what it was really capable of, weren't we? If we just kept our mouths shut, nobody else had to find out, and it wouldn't get used for evil, right?

Chris spoke quietly, as though she had read my mind: "That item—I'm sure some noble family initially purchased it. But then, suddenly, it found its way to the princess. Don't you think that's strange? Who would have given it to the royal family and why?"

There could be only one reason. To switch bodies with the most powerful person in the land...

"Geez, this is no joke. If we don't tell the country's leaders posthaste..."

Chris gave me a sad smile and a slight shake of her head. "I wouldn't recommend it. What do you think they'd do when they found out about the power of the Sacred Treasure? I'll tell you. For starters, every noble in this country would come after the Treasure. For that matter, even the royal family might put it to evil uses. If anything, the more power a person has, the more likely he or she is to crave eternal life."

I couldn't say a word.

Chris went on. "The reason I told you about the Sacred Treasure was because I was confident that even if you got your hands on it, you wouldn't do anything evil with it."

The two of us weren't that close. Why did she trust me so much?

I mean, she wasn't wrong. I didn't have the guts to do anything really bad with an item like that. Even when I switched bodies with Iris, the worst thing I did was try to get into the bath with someone.

...*Wait a second. That seems pretty bad to me...*

As I stood there silently, Chris spoke again. "Hey, aren't you supposed to be the princess's playmate or something?"

Silhouetted by the moonlight, Chris looked at me from the window frame and smiled.

"How about we go have a little playdate at the castle right now?"

Chapter 5

May We Stop These Accursed Plans!

1

Chris and I made for the castle, working our way through the night-cloaked capital.

Chris seemed to think this would be the perfect time for a break-in. Everyone would be so thrilled at having defeated the Demon King's army that the soldiers would let their guard down.

"Hey, whatcha got there? That's kinda neat. Where'd you get it?" Chris asked me. She had covered her mouth with a black cloth.

"A weird employee at a certain magic-item shop in Axel gave this to me. Apparently, it's one of their hottest sellers."

In order to conceal my identity on the off chance we were spotted, I was wearing the mask I'd gotten from Vanir.

"Wow, really? I wouldn't mind having one myself. Who is this weird employee?"

"Good question. His name is Vanir, but apparently he's always diligently keeping the crows away from the trash heap, so the ladies in town call him Vanir the Crow Slayer."

"Huh, he sounds like a real upstanding guy! I'd like to meet him."

She might not think that if she'd actually, y'know, met him. Anyway, I didn't want to imagine what might happen if that demon came face-to-face with a devout Eris follower like Chris.

Our objective was to break in to the castle and steal Iris's necklace.

All the sexual harassment notwithstanding, I had never in my life committed a crime more serious than jaywalking or peeing in an alley, so I was a bit nervous about my first real criminal activity.

I had left my sword at the inn. I didn't want to hurt anybody, and besides, I didn't have the nerve to use it. I had left my chest armor behind, too, the better to run away, and I had changed into black clothes to help me blend in with the night. I did bring my bow, since it could serve a number of uses when it came to infiltration.

Finally, Chris stopped walking. She stood and stared at the castle from a distance.

"Okay, my adorable subordinate, you ready?"

"I'm good anytime, boss lady."

"".........""

"Um, maybe don't call me 'boss lady.'"

"Then don't call me your subordinate. Why do I have to be the lackey anyway?"

Hidden in the shadows, we argued with each other in whispers.

"Look, being a thief is my job. My main class! And your class is Adventurer."

"Yeah, but I'm the one with the Second Sight skill. I'd say that makes me more suited to thief work. Practically speaking, I'm the boss here."

It would hardly do for us to call each other by name while we were breaking into the castle, so we'd spent all night trying to come up with good code names for each other. But so far...

"Hey, I'm the one this whole city knows as 'the righteous thief'! This isn't getting us anywhere. Let's settle this with some kind of contest."

"A contest, huh? Okay. Thieves need Luck. How about a rock, paper, scissors battle with me?"

The one thing that set me apart was my excellent Luck. I didn't think Chris knew about my stats.

"Rock, paper, scissors? Okay, let's go! Come to think of it, I lost to you in a Steal contest a long time ago. Now it's time to pay you back!"

"Ha, I like your spirit, Chris! But I've never lost at rock, paper, scissors. Here we go! Rock! Paper...!"

"First things first, Lowly Assistant. We need to get inside the castle."

"Sure do, Chief. You know, I wasn't just living the NEET life here. I wandered around the castle to kill time, so I've got a good idea of the general layout. I can get us in."

I had lost at rock, paper, scissors for the first time in my life. I guess the Luck of those who worship Eris, goddess of good fortune, was nothing to sneeze at. We each compromised a little and wound up with our current code names.

We had avoided the front gate, which had guards posted at it, and instead worked our way around the castle ramparts.

"This is where we're going to break in, Lowly Assistant? The walls are really high! At least three stories up. Even your lovely friend Chris couldn't—"

Before she finished talking, I pulled out my bow and readied an arrow.

"*Deadeye*!!"

I fired an arrow with a hook at the tip and a rope attached to the shaft, like we'd used in the battle with Destroyer. The skill gave me extra distance and accuracy, and the hook lodged easily on the edge of the rampart.

Chris tugged experimentally on the rope, mouth agape. "You're pretty useful to have around, Lowly Assistant. If you ever quit adventuring, how about you join up with me? We could specialize in stealing from evil rich people."

"If I ever burn through my savings and end up with nothing but time to kill, I'll think about it... All right, let's get started!"

2

It must have been about two or three in the morning. The lights in the castle were out; everyone was asleep.

"I think I'd better go first from here on," I said. "I'll use my night vision, and I'll take it slow. You just follow me, Chief."

"Got it, Lowly Assistant."

At the moment, we were in the castle gardens. Our objective, Iris's room, was on the top floor of the castle.

We encountered our first problem when we reached the door from the gardens into the castle proper.

"Bad news, Chief. The door's locked."

"Let me at it. Get a load of my Lockpick skill." Chris crouched in front of the door and pulled out two objects that looked like ear picks, then inserted them into the keyhole. After a moment, there was a *click*, and the door swung open.

That's a specialist for you. I had some skill points I hadn't used—maybe I would pick up this ability.

Inside the castle, we were plunged into darkness. I led, of course, Chris following close behind me. For now, there weren't even any soldiers patrolling the castle halls. I wondered if things would always go this easily without the luckless Aqua along.

"Let's hide in those shadows over there, Lowly Assistant. Don't forget to activate your Ambush skill."

No sooner had we ducked into the dark corner than we heard the *click-clack* of boots on the floor. A patrol, most likely.

"H-hey, Lowly Assistant, why are you sticking so close to me? We've got Ambush; we don't need to be quite *this* hidden."

"Can't take any chances, Chief. Huddle up now, quick." I pushed Chris deeper into the darkness, keeping very, very close to her.

"Lowly Assistant, I wouldn't mind just a *little* personal space!"

"This is all part of filching the Sacred Treasure and saving the world, Chief. Just roll with it!"

As we argued in whispers, the patrolman came to a halt. "…Is someone there?" he said, raising a lantern. Our Ambush skills must have prevented him from seeing us, because he said, "Just my imagination…?" and resumed his route. I let out a breath.

"Gosh, Chief, didn't I tell you? No chances. If I hadn't been so careful to keep us hidden, we could've been in real trouble there."

"What do you mean?! If you hadn't been talking to me, he never would have noticed us! And if you keep harassing me, one of these days you're going to incur Eris's wrath!"

Shoot! She was right. Eris probably was watching this. Recently, I'd been following my instincts more than even I thought was really appropriate.

I've gotta watch myself.

We worked our way through the sprawling castle, finally arriving at the stairs to the second floor. Iris's room was on the uppermost level. But when I tried to head for it, Chris tugged on my sleeve.

"Hey, Lowly Assistant. If we can, I'd like to hit up the treasure vault here before we go. Like I told you, right? I'm pretty sure there are two Sacred Treasures floating around the capital right now. Really, the only two places I get a major read on treasure are from that guy Alderp and this place."

I still thought she had probably been detecting Aqua's feather mantle at Alderp's mansion. That meant the only other place the second item could be was the castle.

"The treasure room, right. That's on the second floor, just up these stairs. There aren't any guards, but they have a powerful spirit barrier and a bunch of traps…"

"Don't you worry. Traps are one thing I'm ready for."

We went up the stairs, toward the treasure.

The spirit barrier on the door to the treasure room was so powerful that even someone without any particular specialty in magic like me could tell it was there. I figured no one but Aqua could crack it.

But then Chris took some sort of magic item out of her pouch. "Normally, only members of the Crimson Magic Clan have these. It's called a barrier breaker. Some noble had it. I have no idea how they got their hands on it. The Crimson Magic Clan must have sold one. I just thought I'd borrow it."

A barrier breaker? That sounded familiar. In fact, it *looked* familiar... Eh, whatever.

Chris fiddled with the item. It made a *pa-ching!* noise, and the barrier disappeared.

"Wow, that's powerful stuff. I guess now all we have to do is watch out for traps."

"You got it. And both of us have Detect Trap and Disarm Trap, so we really shouldn't have anything to worry about."

I took out my lighter and lit it so we could get our bearings. I shone the dim light around the treasure room, revealing a hoard of neatly stacked loot.

"Oops, traps everywhere. Try to take the treasure, and an alarm will sound. If we don't see the Sacred Treasure we're after, then let's not touch anything."

I nodded in agreement and tried to see if there was anything that looked promising. But really, I didn't know what a monster-summoning Sacred Treasure might look like, so I pretty much had to leave it to Chris and her Sense Treasure skill. For my part, I just kept a lookout, occasionally taking a glance through the piles of treasure...

...and that was when I saw it.

"Okay, Lowly Assistant, it doesn't look like it's here. Lots of powerful magical items, but nothing that would qualify as Sacred— Lowly Assistant?"

It was totally out of place in a room full of treasure.

And to me, it was achingly familiar.

"Comics...!"

A manga magazine was lying there. It could only have been brought from Japan.

As I looked at the book with unmistakable nostalgia, Chris must have known something was running through my mind, because she watched me closely.

"Um… If you try to take that…"

She couldn't quite bring herself to say it, but I knew what she meant. "It's okay. That book is from my country. I was just thinking how much I miss the place."

For some reason, this caused Chris to adopt an apologetic expression.

"You don't have to look at me like that," I said. "Anyway, I actually owned that comic, so I don't especially—"

I was in the middle of my sentence when I noticed the book sitting next to the manga. It was the utmost treasure. Something that people in Japan might jump you just to get, if you were so lucky as to have one.

"Ready to go, Lowly Assistant? …Oh! Once we seal the Sacred Treasures, maybe I'll get you some books from your home country. So let's…"

Chris was jabbering on about something, but I didn't hear her. I was too focused on getting that treasure.

"Lowly Assistant—!!"

"There! The intruders went that way!"

"Two intruders! We don't know what they're after, but don't let them go any farther!"

Chris and I ran for our lives, the soldiers' shouts ringing in our ears.

"Damn! What a fiendish trap! To think, it got even me…!"

"When we get out of this, you and I are going to have a long talk, Lowly Assistant! You're just too impetuous!"

"Chief, now's not the time to argue! We've gotta find a way out of here!"

"Don't you tell me that! I'm well aware!"

Lights were coming on all over the castle. The alarm from the vault must have woken people up.

"*Create Water*! And *Freeze*!" I laid down ice in the hallway as we ran. A moment later, shouts and cries came from behind us.

"You really are good to have around, Lowly Assistant."

"Cut the chatter, Chief, and just think of a way to help us!"

Chris had come up to jog alongside me as we traded banter, and she gave me a thumbs-up. "You got it! Let your chief show you what she can do!"

Then Chris spun around, producing something from her pocket: thin pieces of metal wire.

"*Wire Trap*!" she shouted as she flung them.

When the little pieces of wire touched the walls, they instantly spread out into a steel net, like a spiderweb. Even a small person would have had trouble squeezing through it.

"That should buy us enough time to escape. What with all the commotion, Lowly Assistant, I think we'd better call it a night. What say we get out of here?" Chris drew a dagger from the small of her back as she spoke and used it to punch out a window. She was looking around the area, ready to run.

"No, wait. Whatever I can do today, I'd like to do it! They're going to kick me out of the capital tomorrow!"

Chris gave me a pained look. "I-I'm sorry, but… A Thief and an Adventurer? If we tried to take them on, they'd arrest us in no time at all. And when did you get so resolute anyway?!"

Her words made me think. Why *was* I so desperate to do this? I wasn't the hot-blooded character, and I definitely wasn't the "chosen one" hero type.

Just calm down. I'm cooler than this.

Yeah. If I went back to Axel, I could have my life of leisure. I didn't need to do this. I could just run away and relax at my mansion…

That was what I kept trying to tell myself anyway, but my days with Iris kept flashing before my eyes.

Iris in a bad mood when I teased her. Iris with her eyes shining as she listened to my story of purifying a Lich in a dungeon. Iris after I had convinced her to sneak some food from the dining hall, looking embarrassed but also somehow happy as Claire scolded us both. Iris crying and yelling at me after she had happily repeated to her servants some outrageous lie I'd told her.

And then there were the words she'd said to me when I asked her why she would ever like me.

"I've never met anyone like you before. I've had lots of servants, but there was no one who was totally fearless, and rude, and obnoxious, and willing to tell a princess like me all kinds of dirty things, and who wanted to win at any cost in a totally immature way..."

I didn't think any of that was actually a compliment, but still...

"I was trying to find out why you would *like me."*

"And that's what I'm talking about, isn't it?"

She really liked me...for me.

I didn't know how I'd gotten in so deep. I definitely didn't know why I was so fond of Iris. I mean, in a few years she would be a princess of marriageable age. And then there was no chance that she would be allowed to keep meeting with a guy who was not only so much lower in social status but as suspicious as I was.

In fact, the moment I left this castle, there would be nothing to connect us anymore. So tonight was my last chance to act like a big brother to her.

"Lowly Assistant, I really think we should get out of here! You go back to Axel—it might take me a while on my own, but I'll do something about the Sacred Treasure!"

But that was exactly why...

"Chief, I..."

I had been through the wringer already. I couldn't make any promises about the future. I could barely make any promises about the next day.

*   *   *

But—

"Now, right now, I can do what I need to do."

"Lowly Assistant…?"

"There! We're through the wire! But the thieves…didn't get away; they're still standing right there for some reason!"

The soldiers had cut through Chris's wire trap, and now there was nothing between us and them.

One guy, apparently their leader, was bellowing, "You villains! You'll regret coming to our castle! Make sure we take one alive—then we'll find out what they're after!"

One of the soldiers who stood blocking our way reported back to the shouting man, "Captain! One of them has a dagger, but the other one seems to be unarmed. Let's try for the weakling with no weapon!"

The captain nodded. "I agree, the silver-haired one looks strong. All right, give the silver-haired intruder no quarter! But two of you should be more than enough for the weak-looking guy in the mask!"

What's with me tonight?

Was it because I had genuinely decided to be serious this one time?

"We're dealing with a criminal here! I don't need him in one piece!"

I was on top of my game.

"They're not moving. You, intruders! If you're going to surrender, now's your chance. You *might* get away with your lives!"

For some reason, I was actually on top of my game tonight.

The captain was pointing his sword at me.

"……"

I didn't say anything but raised my hand, almost as if I were going to shake his. He lowered the weapon slightly in puzzlement.

"Oh-ho. Waving the white flag? Good. You, Silver Hair, throw down your weapon! If you do, we miiiiiaggghhhh!"

The moment he took my hand, he screamed and crumpled to the ground, twitching.

""""Huh?!"""""

Everyone else, including Chris, looked at one another and voiced their amazement.

The man they were calling "captain" seemed to be made of fairly stern stuff. But besides Darkness, who had the strength of a monster, there weren't many people who could withstand my Drain Touch when I was in my groove.

"Wh-what did he do?!" The other soldiers took a step back, their captain still lying on the floor.

"Bwa-ha-ha-ha-ha-ha! Perfect! I've never felt better! I don't know why, but I'm in top form! And tonight, you're going to see what happens when I get *really* serious!"

"L-Lowly Assistant? You've been acting really weird! Are you okay?"

I jumped at the remaining soldiers!

3

"Chief! The stairs to the top floor are just to the right around that corner!"

"S-sure, got it! B-but look, Lowly Assistant, you sound...and are acting...totally different from normal. What's going on?!"

Chris and I continued to hear shouting behind us as we ran along. The difference from earlier was...

"Thieves! Extremely capable thieves have broken in! Call our best adventurers!"

"Be on the alert—do not try to engage them alone! They're very powerful! They don't seem to want to kill anyone for the moment, but don't let your guard down!"

"Knight captain, this way! Please evacuate to safety!"

"B-but that masked man—I can't allow him to go any farther!"

The difference was that I was pumped, and the soldiers seemed oddly afraid of me.

Whoops, enemy detected in front!

"Okay, step aside! Silver-Haired Thief Brigade coming through! If you don't want to get hurt, then get out of the way!"

"When did we agree on a name, Lowly Assistant?! This is getting serious—let's call it the Masked Thief Brigade, and you can be the leader!"

The soldier ahead of us had his sword out.

"*Wind Breath!*"

"Gwah?! Curse him and his little parlor tricks— Ahhhh!"

My wind magic blew the fine soil from my palm into his face. I grabbed the hand of my blinded opponent, holding his sword at bay while I drained him. Within seconds of touching the soldier, I had rendered him helpless. I walked away as if nothing had happened.

"The Masked Thief Brigade? No thanks. It makes me sound like the ringleader."

"Hey, I don't want the villain treatment, either! I wasn't exactly eager to become public enemy number one, but now everyone's gonna recognize me by the color of my hair! And what's that skill you keep using anyway?!"

I could hardly admit to using Lich skills. "This is my secret finishing move. And because it's secret, I can't tell you anything about it. Bigger problem: If they bring out anyone who can use magic, I won't have a leg to stand on… And speak of the devil, that looks like a wizard now! You're up, Chief!"

We were faced with three soldiers who had apparently just jumped out of bed. Two of them wore armor, but one was wearing a robe.

"You got it! I'll handle him with my skills somehow…! *Skill Bind!*"

Chris activated her skill before the robed soldier could finish chanting his spell.

"*Lightning*! …H-huh?"

His spell's failure to activate threw him for a loop. I pulled out a piece of rope as I ran and shouted, "*Bind*!"

I flung the rope at the two soldiers. Imbued with magic power by the skill, it wrapped itself around them as though it had a mind of its own. I was really glad Chris had taught me that skill. It was proving very useful. The only bottleneck was how much MP such a powerful ability consumed…

I closed the distance with one of the bound men, then used Drain Touch to steal as much MP as he could survive. I had used up most of my own magic on Bind, but now I was topped right up.

The soldiers yelled and shouted:

"He beat us again! He doesn't even have a weapon! What the hell is he?!"

"Where are the adventurers?! Aren't our adventurers here yet?!"

"W-well… We served our best wine at the party, so most of them drank themselves into oblivion…"

"This is why I hate adventurers!"

That little exchange brought me a rush of relief. If we'd really had to face off with high-level adventurers, we could have been in a tight spot.

"Our knights and soldiers are vulnerable to Thief skills! Isn't there anything we can do?!"

"Normally, you don't get too much mileage out of Bind; it takes too much MP. Maybe that guy has a whole bunch of manatite or something…?"

"But we never saw him using any! Which would mean…"

"That thief has a terrifying amount of MP! As much as a member of the Crimson Magic Clan!"

The soldiers behind me were letting their imaginations run away with them, making me sound a lot more powerful than I was. I was just using Drain Touch conscientiously.

And eventually…

"Wha—?! Crap, don't let them get to the top floor! We don't know what they're after, but Princess Iris is up there…!"

We were heading for the top floor, where Iris was.

"*Wire Trap! Wire Trap! Wire Trap!!*" Chris riddled the stairway with wires. She let out a sigh of relief. "All right, that oughta keep them off our tails for a while! Now we just—"

"Now you just get captured and tell us what it is you want here. Who or what are you? Are you the righteous thief—or thieves—of the rumors?"

We turned around to find Mitsurugi in full regalia. And with him…

"You've cut off your own escape route. Consider yourselves finished, intruders!"

That declaration came from Claire and Lain, looking their absolute most dangerous.

At a distance stood an audience of nobles and a whole bunch of knights.

4

"What are we going to do, Lowly Assistant? I don't think we can take on all these people at once!" Chris whispered to me with a squeak.

A quick glance suggested Lain was the only magic user. Mitsurugi was up front, hesitantly closing the distance along with the knights behind him, who had their swords drawn. Behind them, Claire was watching us with a triumphant look on her face. The other nobles seemed to be enjoying the show, too, apparently convinced that this was already over.

"Miss Claire," Mitsurugi said, "that masked man is supposed to be very powerful. He doesn't seem to have a weapon, but if he gets close to you, there's no telling what he might do. I'll handle him. Knights, you take the boy with the silver hair."

"…You know, Lowly Assistant, people keep calling me 'kid' and 'boy' here. All I've done is cover my mouth. Does it make me look that much like a guy?"

"I don't think it's your mouth, Chief, so much as your flat ch— Yikes! Now is no time to be getting upset, Chief. We're going to need everything we've got."

I tried to backpedal as I saw Chris's face fall practically before my eyes. Then I turned toward Mitsurugi. He had his enchanted blade close and wasn't taking his eyes off me.

"Okay, Chief. At times like this, you knock out the most powerful enemy to scare the rest. I'm in top form tonight—I'll drop that empty-headed hunk like a sack of bricks. Then we make our escape while everyone else is frozen in terror."

"Y-you know I can hear you, right? 'Empty-headed hunk'? You mean me? And 'sack of bricks'? Quite the talk for someone who isn't carrying a weapon. Very well, I'll give you everything I've—"

While Mitsurugi was still babbling away, I raised my hand toward his sword. He saw me and dropped into a deep stance, his hand on his scabbard, ready to draw.

He was an advanced class and a high-level adventurer. Stealing his sword and using Drain Touch on him would keep me busy for a few minutes.

"What's that gesture? Steal? Too bad for you. Someone once defeated me using Steal, and ever since then I've carried around lots of junk as a countermeasure. Now, if you'll just come quietly—"

"*Freeze!*"

I intoned my ice magic over Mitsurugi as he spoke. It was just Basic Magic, so Mitsurugi, sensing an attempt at a diversion, kept his eye on me and didn't budge an inch. I walked casually up to him…

"What do you think you're doing? Try this on for s—?!"

He tried to pull out his sword but was stunned to find the hilt had been frozen to the scabbard and he couldn't get it out. I took the instantaneous window of opportunity to grab Mitsurugi by the nose and mouth with one hand.

"*Create Water!*"

"*Glub?!*"

Mitsurugi clawed at my hand in a panic as water materialized inside his mouth and he started to drown where he stood.

"Do you admit your defeat?" I called out. "Will you stand down?"

Even as Mitsurugi gasped for breath, he gritted his teeth and made a fist...

"*Freeze!*"

"Hrk?!"

Before he could raise it, though, I turned the water in his mouth and nose to solid ice.

"Master Mitsurugi!" Claire screamed. I let him go and he fell to his knees, clutching his throat.

"If you hurry and melt the ice, he *probably* won't suffocate. Come on, anyone else think they're stronger than him? ...Chief, now! Away we go!"

"I can never tell if you're really weak or really strong. But I know I wouldn't want you as an enemy."

The knights, intimidated by how I had made good on my threat to topple Mitsurugi in a flash, backed away. As Chris offered one of her usual quips, the two of us threaded our way past them.

"Lain, do something about the ice in Master Mitsurugi's throat—be a little rough if you have to! And you, what are you all doing?! How can there be so many of you and not one of you can land a blow? Master Mitsurugi may be out of the fight—but that doesn't mean you should just let them through!"

"But their Evade is so high—they must have the Flee skill! If they focus completely on running away...! All right, everyone, split into two groups! The thieves can't possibly know the castle as well as we do! You guys, go around the other way!"

"Everyone, please calm down! The thieves will soon be caught—so please, just stay calm!"

As we approached, the nobles blanched and started running this way and that, hindering the knights. We took advantage of the confusion to use Bind on some of the knights in our way. The guards seemed to think we wouldn't know the terrain, but I hadn't just been wasting time wandering around the castle. If we could only get through here, then…!

"Lowly Assistant, behind us! Someone's coming!"

At Chris's warning, I looked back and saw that Lain had finished tending to Mitsurugi. Now she had her staff pointed at us and was intoning some magic spell.

Claire was in a panic. "Princess Iris is just up ahead! We can't let them keep going—even if it means killing them! If worse comes to worst, Lady Aqua can use her Resurrection spell! So don't hold back, Lain!"

The jewel on the end of Lain's staff began to glow with a strange light. I grabbed the bow off my back, took aim at the end of the staff, and let it fly.

"*Deadeye!*"

"Yeek!" Lain gave a little shout and stopped moving as the gem shattered.

Claire and the knights stood dumbfounded.

"Who *is* that masked man anyway?! And why would such a capable person become a thief?!" I could hear Claire groaning in frustration as we dashed away.

5

"Iris's room is just up ahead. Kindly put a wire trap here, Chief."

"You got it, Lowly Assistant. Just one, though. I'm getting a little tight on magic."

We had come out into the corridor that led to Iris's room, and now we set a trap to stymie the pursuing knights. Using Flee to its maximum potential had gained us a lot of distance, leaving our pursuers quite a ways behind us. We stood before the door to the princess's room. I opened it…

*   *   *

"I'm impressed you made it this far, intruders. Protecting the people, protecting the country, and protecting the royal family—these are the duties of the Dustiness household. As long as I'm here—"

I closed it again.

"Don't close the door on me! Why are you even here—?!"
Darkness pulled the door open with a bang, but when she saw us, she stopped dead.
She didn't know it was us yet! She didn't know!
"Ch-Ch-Chief! Don't just stand there trembling; we've got a job to do! I know how powerful this big, intimidating female knight looks, but don't let her scare you! We have to do this—for the good of the nation!"
"Y-y-y-you're right, Lowly Assistant! This is for the good of the nation, and although we can't tell anyone about it, it's the right thing!"
"So it is, Chief! Because no one else realizes the princess is wearing an exceedingly dangerous item! Gosh! If we hadn't shown up, she could have been in real trouble!"
Darkness's frown deepened as we delivered this exposition thinly disguised as banter. But it was okay! She still didn't know who we were!
"Let's go into the room together, Lowly Assistant! After that, we can both apologize!"
"When you're right, you're right! I'm one hundred percent sure they'll understand when we explain what was going on!"
"H-hey...! Y-y-you two..."
"Darkness, what's going on? Didn't I tell you the tone you take at the beginning of a battle is of utmost importance?"
She was hidden behind Darkness, but apparently Megumin was there, too.
"Stand aside. I can detain a thief or two! My MP hasn't regenerated enough for me to use magic yet, but I am confident in my fisti-

cuffs! In fact, earlier this very day I took on three thugs and won, so I'm sure...I...can..."

Megumin had her staff at the ready, but when she saw us as we shoved our way into the room, she stopped moving.

Okay! This is okay! Megumin's a smart cookie. Even if she realizes who we are...

"S-so cool...!"

...then if we just explain how dangerous Iris's divine item is, she'll... Wait, what?

As she looked at my face, Megumin was blushing and trembling.

"What shall we do, Darkness? Surely this is the righteous thief! Who else would put on such a cool outfit and dress all in black to boot? What's your name?! Have you decided the name of your thief gang yet?!"

She really *didn't* know who we were.

"...Y-you accursed thieves... Um, now you'll face the—uh, the Dustiness family's..."

Darkness sounded like she was reading from a script; she stood with her sword ready but without much conviction. Apparently, she'd figured out what we were here for and was going to cooperate with us. Her clenched fist was shaking, like she was struggling to endure something.

What to do, what to do? I guess I'll explain to her later. But in the meantime, to make things more believable, I'd better tie her up.

"*Bind*!"

As the rope wrapped itself around her, I thought I saw Darkness let out a little sigh, relief on her face. Now she had an excuse for not fighting back...

Aqua's voice echoed through the room. "*Sacred Dispel*!"

Darkness was the target of the spell; the rope dropped limply to the floor.

"It's your bad luck I was here, huh?!" Aqua appeared from deeper in the room, still protectively clutching her bottle of booze. "I don't have any idea what you want, but when I bring you in, I'm sure to get another bottle of great wine! As you can see, your skills are useless in the face of my power! Now, come quietly!"

Damn it all! Why did she have to pick now to start being useful? It makes me so angry! Why can she never, ever take a hint about what's going on?!

"Now, Darkness! Get them! Megumin seems to have gone brain-dead—so you're our only hope!"

Free from Bind thanks to Aqua, Darkness had no choice but to raise her sword again, practically crying. Knights' footsteps were approaching.

"Chief! Thanks to that idiot, we can't stay here any longer! Iris is in here! Let's find her, and I'll Steal—!"

"Steal the Sacred Treasure! Great thinking! But…your Steal…"

True. Against female targets, my Steal had an unusually high chance of coming up with a pair of panties.

Then we heard the shouting behind us.

"Cut through the wire, quick! The thieves are after Princess Iris!"

We were out of time. It was possible I'd wound Iris in the process, but I'd do anything to increase my chances of nabbing the Sacred Treasure.

"Y-you fiends shall not stand against my m-mighty sidesweep!" bellowed Darkness before taking a pitifully weak swipe at us. I ducked under her sword, and Chris and I headed farther into the room.

"D'oh, Darkness, why do you have to be so dumb?! You don't *announce* what attack you're going to use! This is why everyone calls you a muscle head!"

"*…Sniffle.*"

A tear came into Darkness's eye as she received a scolding from the real dumb one, the person who least understood what was going on here. Beside them, Megumin was watching me as if I were a hero at work.

And then, from farther into the room—just where we were headed—Iris appeared, holding a bejeweled rapier low in her right hand, her left hand outstretched. And on that left hand was a ring, and the ring was letting off some kind of white light, and the light was getting brighter…!

"Intruders! I am a member of the royal family. Know that I, too, have inherited the blood of heroes, and their power runs in my veins! I will not be easily carried…off…"

She had been ready to fight like a tiger, but when she saw us, Iris's eyes went wide. The glow from the ring faded, and her voice grew small.

This was our chance!

""*Steal*!!"" Chris and I shouted together, hoping to steal something Iris was wearing.

At the same moment, Claire shouted from behind us, "Your Highness! Are you all right?!"

Damn! No time to see if we stole the right thing!

"Let's jump to the terrace from here, Lowly Assistant! Our good luck—there's a pool right under it! If we just take a leap of faith…!" Chris, holding something, hustled past Iris.

"It was only logical that that's where you would go! I don't know what you have there, but I won't let you take it!"

Aqua reached out her hand toward us.

This damn goddess, dense to the very end!

"*Seal*—!!"

"Damn it allll!"

Chris and I tried to get a bead on the pitch-black pool as we jumped.

To Become a True Big Brother

The morning of the next day. As dawn came, the capital was in an uproar. And why shouldn't it be? The "righteous thief" had broken into the castle and, with a crew of just two people, stolen a magic item from the princess. And on a night when a bunch of powerful adventurers were staying there, to boot.

The story of the smash-and-grab by a silver-haired boy and a masked man spread like wildfire.

Which brought us to now. The capital as a whole wasn't the only place full of commotion. So was the room I was in.

"D-D-D-D-Darkness, calm dooowwnnn! I swear there's a perfectly good explanation if you'll just— Yowww! My head! My head's gonna come clean off!"

"Yeah, listen to us already! Just let us explain, and you'll say, *Oh, now I understand exactly why they did it!* Please! I'm gonna die any minute here!"

"Oh, I'll listen! You'd better believe I want to hear what your excuse is this time. I'm just blowing off some steam first. Since you claim to have a good reason, I won't squeeze with *all* my strength yet!"

Chris and I, answering a summons from Darkness, were in a room at the inn, getting a taste of her Iron Talon.

"Darkness! D-Darkness! I can't talk… I can't t-talk like this!"

"Stoppit! Chris dragged me into it; she's the one you want! She's the chief, the mastermind!"

Darkness had one hand on my temple and another on Chris's, and she was squeezing. She looked startlingly serious.

"Wh-wh-why, you impossible—! Eeeyow, ow, ow, ow! N-no, Darkness, listen! My lowly assistant was totally into it! It's true I'm the one who came up with the idea, but when things turned ugly, *I* said we should get out of there—he was the one who decided to keep going!"

"Wrong, Chief, wrong! I've only been in the Righteous Thief Brigade for one day; I'm definitely at the bottom of the ranks!"

"Quit calling it that! It's not a brigade; it's just the two of us! And that means there are no 'ranks'!"

Still grasping our temples, Darkness had forced us to sit formally on the floor, where each of us proceeded to enthusiastically blame the other. Darkness was watching us, angrier than I'd ever seen her.

"All right."

""?!""

Darkness's icy voice cut through our argument.

"Talk. Fast."

Between us, we explained how it had all happened.

After she had heard us out, Darkness heaved a sigh.

"…What am I going to do with you two? Why didn't you tell me? If you had come to me to begin with, you wouldn't have had to pull that ridiculous stunt. I would've listened to you."

"I appreciate it, but we're talking about a Sacred Treasure that lets you switch bodies. It could even be used to gain eternal life. When I heard about it, I wanted to run to the authorities, but Chris warned me that the more powerful the person, the more they would want it. Even the royal family might misuse it."

"I—I said I thought we could trust you, Darkness! But when I tried to tell you, my lowly assistant was all, 'Hey, stop! Darkness is a noble, too. If the other nobles find out you're the thief, she could be in real trouble!'"

"Hey! Wh-why, you—!"

As our feud started up again, Darkness let out another sigh. "What's done is done. Thankfully, I'm the only one who's figured out who you really are so far. Chris, your silver hair draws too much attention. You need to get out of the capital immediately and head back to Axel. As for you, Kazuma... You're coming to the castle with me right now."

"What?! ...Argh! My head really hurts where you had a grip on it! Sorry, but I'm going to stay here and rest."

"Quit playing these stupid games and come with me! We have to go get Megumin and Aqua and say our good-byes to Princess Iris!"

"Yeah, I get it, but the castle's still on high alert. I don't know about walking right in... I might screw up again. Or what if they suspect me, and they bring out one of those bells that rings when you lie? It'd be bad news!"

Chris scratched her cheek and gave me a friendly smile as I crossed my arms and Darkness started dragging me away.

"Well, s-see you then, Lowly Assistant. Fight the good fight! Oh, and the Sacred Treasure we took? I put it somewhere no one would ever find it, so you don't have to worry about that. I—I guess I'll show myself out, then..."

"Hold on, Chris," Darkness said.

"?! Y-yes, what is it?"

"Is that everything you're hiding from me? You're not holding back anything else?"

"...Well, um..."

"You are, aren't you?! What is it? What aren't you telling me?! We've known each other a long time—long enough that I can tell when you're feeling cornered! You scratch that scar on your cheek—just like you're doing now! Spit it out! What are you hiding this time?"

Chris, reeling from this barrage of questions, looked to me for help for some reason. But I had no idea what it was she wasn't telling Darkness, so I couldn't do anything—

Then she pointed at me.

"My lowly assistant—he stole something besides the Sacred Treasure!"

"Whaaaat?! You traitor!"

"You stole something else?! So you really are just a common thief! What did you take?! Hand it over!"

Resigned, I slowly handed over a book. Darkness skimmed through it.

"You impossible…" She seemed to crumple a little.

Chris muttered, "Oh yeah… I forgot you grabbed that, too."

"Huh?"

"…Oh-ho? There's more?" Darkness stood up again and stretched out her hand to me.

What other treasure did I steal? What could she possibly…?

"Wait, I get it! Geez, you meant this? The thing I got when I used Steal on Iris?"

As I spoke, I gave Darkness the item I had stolen from the princess. It was a ring she'd been wearing. Given the way it had glowed when she'd pointed it at Chris and me, it was probably some kind of magical item.

For a moment, Darkness held it in the palm of her hand, frowning intently at it. "…?! You—you… Y-y-you took this from Princess Iris?!"

"Y-yeah… I mean, what's with the reaction? It's even scarier than if you were mad at me! I mean, it's just a ring, right? Don't scare me, okay?"

Darkness stared distantly at the ring a moment longer, then carefully passed it back to me.

"Listen to me, Kazuma. Do *not* lose this ring. Take it to your grave, where no one will ever find it."

"Quit it already! I-if it's that big a deal, we can go give it back right now. Say we found it someplace."

"Out of the question! This is a ring given to children of the royal family on the day they're born. It never leaves them—not when they're sleeping, not when they're bathing. The only time they remove it is when they get engaged and they give it to their betrothed. If word got out that a thief stole it and some adventurer picked it up…! …Even if you returned it with the best of intentions, they would probably kill you, just to make sure nobody else would ever know."

"Yikes! Way to freak me out. Hey, Chris! Where do you think you're going? You're the one who got me into this mess. Sneak into Iris's room and put this back!"

"No way! I'm scared! Why does your Steal always take the worst possible things? And Darkness, you've changed. When did you start hiding evidence? I remember how dense you used to be, but I guess you've learned something about getting by in the world… I can't shake the sense that you've been corrupted by my lowly assistant."

"Wha…?! H-hang on—I know I'm not very self-aware, but have I really changed that much?! I'm more worried about the princess being corrupted…"

Apparently, this was all shocking to her. I ignored the other two, holding the ring up to the light.

"…No choice, I guess. When we get home, I'll bury it in the garden or something. I don't think anyone will find it there."

"Don't be stupid! That ring was Princess Iris's precious possession! You have to take care of it—don't ever be without it! And also don't ever let anyone see it!"

"What sort of twisted game is this?! Ahhh, fine, I get it. Give me back my other treasure, too. I mean, it's too late to return that one, either, right?"

"……"

Chris and Darkness looked at each other.

When Darkness and I arrived at the castle, I was like one of the walking dead, courtesy of the living hell I'd been through.

"Come on, stop shuffling! You can't slump in front of the princess!"

"*Sniff…sniff…* Whyyyy? Why'd you have to burn it…? I saved this country and nobody even knew… It was my one reward…"

"Get over yourself. You look pathetic. That 'lighter' or whatever of yours sure came in handy. Yeah… I could see this being useful."

"I didn't make it to do *that*, though! *Sniff…sniff…* My treasure…!"

I'd meant to keep the book for myself, but the two of them had burned it in front of me. I couldn't summon the energy to do anything at all.

Chris said she was going to make herself scarce before somebody decided to be a hero and arrest the silver-haired thief. She said she would come back to Axel when she was good and ready, so I'd probably see her again. Maybe it hadn't worked out so well, but I actually enjoyed partnering up with her, just a little. *When they find out who I am and put out an arrest warrant for me, maybe we really should form a Righteous Thief Brigade.*

All this was running through my mind as I followed Darkness through the castle. Finally, she stopped in front of Iris's room.

"…It'll only be trouble if I bring you in there looking like you do now. I'll explain about the Sacred Treasure. You just wait here."

"What'd you even bring me for, then? I'm not in a very good mood right now. If you dragged me all the way out here just to leave me standing in a hallway, I might end up wandering the castle, and who knows what I'd do then?"

"What are you, a kid?! Fine, but don't cause any trouble! I plan to explain the dangers of the Sacred Treasure and tell them that the righteous thief's goal was to save Princess Iris—it's almost the truth. If you screw this up, believe me, it won't go easy for you!"

I shoved past Darkness as she blathered on and opened the door to the room.

"You stupid, stupid—! What kind of person doesn't even knock?! …Your Highness, it's me! Lalatina! We need to talk to you, urgently!"

Darkness and I entered the room to find…

"Well, it was easy peasy for me! I sealed that Sacred Treasure right up, and now no one can use it again. So relax! Sheesh, those thieves didn't know what they were in for!"

"As a member of the Crimson Magic Clan, expert in all things magical, I offer my assurances as well. That was quite the impressive Sacred Treasure, but no one else can use it now. In other words, this case is open-and-shut!"

Aqua and Megumin stood there in front of Iris and her entourage, looking awfully pleased with themselves despite the fact that they didn't really do much this time.

Lain breathed a sigh and said with a relieved smile, "Nothing less from Miss Aqua and Miss Megumin! That really puts my mind at ease. When you told me about the item's true power, Miss Aqua, I was as pale as a ghost!"

"But what do you think those burglars wanted? Their reputation among the populace wouldn't suggest they meant to misuse the item, but… Hmm? Lady Dustiness and…*you.*"

Claire, for her part, didn't sound any nicer than usual.

Aqua, it appeared, had already told them how dangerous the Sacred Treasure was.

"I investigated that Sacred Treasure and learned that it is in fact immensely dangerous. We came to warn you, but it looks like there's no need," Darkness said, apparently relieved not to have to go through with her little act.

Then, from the center of the clump of people, Iris spoke. "Do you suppose those two came to help me? That they knew about the necklace's true power and believed that if they made the danger known, someone might put it to evil purposes?" For some reason, she was staring right at me as she spoke.

Is this the part where it turns out she knows the thief's true identity?

"Your Highness, I'm sure you're overthinking it. I know they call those thieves righteous, but even a burglar with a conscience wouldn't deliberately put himself in danger just for something like that." Claire closed her eyes, almost regretfully. "If one did, I would have to admit he was a very impressive man." A note of respect mingled with the regret. Claire had become pretty much my least favorite person, but I couldn't help feeling a bit of newfound affection for her at this.

"Who do you suppose those two really were, though?" Lain asked. "I like to think I'm well acquainted with our higher-level adventurers, but I can't think of anyone quite as capable as them. Especially that masked man... I only faced him for a moment, but he was able to destroy my staff from a great distance."

Yikes. I love a good pat on the back, but this is getting awkward.

"Yes! That masked man!" Megumin said. "He was very cool, was he not? That mask and black outfit—a man after my own heart! Next time I see him, I must get an autograph!"

"M-Miss Megumin, you might remember that we're talking about a criminal! ...But I have to admit, he was something else. He stopped Master Mitsurugi in the blink of an eye, to say nothing of about half the royal knights, even though he wasn't so much as carrying a weapon..."

Megumin and Claire both sighed wistfully.

Well, crap. What do I do? I really want to brag that it was me all along.

"Kazuma, what's going on? That smirk on your face is giving me the creeps." Aqua was still cradling the bottle of wine. One of these days I was going to have to take it from her.

Aqua's words caused Claire to fix me with a glare. "She's right. What *are* you grinning about? You missed your big chance to catch the thief. Not that I think you would have lasted a minute against that masked man. Ah... Why did someone like that have to become a thief? If only he wasn't a criminal, he would be more than welcome here... I wish I could meet him again..." She blushed ever so slightly as she said this, the first girlish act of behavior I had ever seen from her.

So was she going to condemn me or praise me to the heavens? I wished she would make up her mind.

...Then Iris threw in her two cents: "Yes, that righteous thief really was manly, wasn't he?" As she spoke, she fixed me with a stare.

Wait a second. What's going on here? She really must have figured it out...right?

"This is just my own flight of fancy," Iris said, "but I'm convinced those two thieves really did do all that because they were worried for me. I'm afraid I may have…fallen rather in love…"

Okay. Definitely time to reveal my true identity.

Darkness noticed me digging in my bag, ready to pull out the mask, and made a vigorous finger-across-the-throat gesture to cut me off. I was about to hit her with Drain Touch to keep her out of my way, when—

"I wonder where he is now? My silver-haired chief…!"

I let my hand drop back to my side. Of course that was who she was talking about!

Iris looked at me as I stood there, frozen. Her face flushed. She lowered her eyes to the ground, her narrow shoulders shaking.

…Hey, she's not laughing, is she?

Then the shaking stopped, and she looked up again. She saw my irritation. Her voice trembled just a bit:

"E-Elder Brother. May I ask…one thing of you?"

"Y-Your Highness?" Claire seemed confused by the electrified atmosphere.

Other than dragging me here in the first place, Iris had never shown any sign of selfishness toward me. Now her fist was clenched, her face serious, as though she had come to some decision.

But just as she was about to speak, Darkness said, "Your Highness. Before you make your wish known, there's something I want to say to you."

Everyone looked at her. Darkness dropped to one knee but shot a glance at me. "This man, Kazuma Satou, has bested many generals of the Demon King. It may even be he who one day defeats the Demon King himself. It is an immensely difficult task, one no ordinary person could achieve… Please, when you speak, bear in mind the challenges he already faces."

Whoa, where had this come from? She thought I might defeat *what*?

"Defeat the Demon King? Really? Elder Brother, do you truly seek to topple the evil ruler?" Iris, too, seemed completely serious.

No, I don't! That's obviously completely impossi—

"Well, uh, I mean, if the opportunity comes up, then maybe...I could, you know...think about it? I guess?"

I couldn't do it. I couldn't say it to her face.

Behind her, Claire snorted as if this was the stupidest thing she had ever heard.

But...

"I see... I'm sure you can do it, Elder Brother. Please give everything you've got to defeating the Demon King. I wish you every success!"

And then Iris smiled as wide as the sky, and no one was able to say anything at all.

I take that back. One person was.

"Elder Brother this, Elder Brother that! Why don't you just stop it already? You have an actual elder brother, you know! Get all sweet and cozy with *him*! I can't help feeling oddly threatened by that form of address! One day *I* am going to bury the Demon King—Kazuma need not even be there!"

It was Megumin, who was very worked up for some reason.

"W-well, Elder Brother is Elder Brother! If I call Elder Brother 'Elder Brother,' what's wrong with that? And anyway, it would be point-less for you to defeat the Demon King; I want Elder Brother to do it!"

"I told you to stop using that name, and you immediately used it five times! That amounts to throwing down the gauntlet!"

"Y-you wanna go?! I'm w-warning you, the royal family is very strong!"

Darkness and Claire rushed to separate them before things could get any worse.

"Quit it, Megumin! Weren't you best friends with Princess Iris just the other day? And now you're starting a fight?! What's gotten into you?"

"Your Highness, please calm down! You've never even been in a fight before—what's gotten into you?"

I tried to calm her down by changing the subject. "So what was it you wanted to ask me for? Go ahead, anything at all."

I was actually pretty curious. What with the way she'd been acting, maybe she would ask me to stay in the castle…!

"Oh yeah… My wish…"

She was the one who had brought it up in the first place, but now she paused, almost as if she had to think about it.

"Our game isn't over yet. I hope you'll have another round with me sometime."

And then she smiled like a mischievous little girl.

The Voracious Noble and the Broken Demon

I could hear an occasional asthmatic wheezing in the musty basement. An unsettling sound, every time.

"Max? Get up, Max!"

I gave the wheezing form a swift kick, and he sat up as if nothing had happened.

"*Wheeze...wheeze...* O-oh, it's you, Alderp. Need something from me? Ahh, you're letting off a lovely aura today, as always, Alderp."

He was mocking me—it was obvious. Almost without thinking, I kicked the demon again.

A demon: Yes, that's what this disgusting thing was.

At first glance, he appeared to be a young man, his features almost intimidatingly shapely, but his expressionless face, as if drained of all emotion, never failed to send nameless shivers running down my spine.

"Why would I ever come down here if I *didn't* need something from you? I have a job for you. Some thief stole my Sacred Treasure and sealed it up, to boot. I want you to get it back and break the seal. Understand?"

"*Wheeze...wheeze...* Alderp, Alderp! That's impossible, Alderp! I don't even know where it is, and normally it's impossible to seal a Sacred Treasure. If it was really sealed, then I have no chance of— Hrk?!"

As he blathered excuses at me, I kicked him again.

"Are you saying you can't even do this, you worthless lout?! When exactly *will* you be able to grant my wish? Lalatina! Hurry up and bring me Lalatina! Why is that so hard?!"

"*Wheeze...wheeze...wheeze...wheeze...*"

Again and again I kicked him; he covered his disgusting face and curled into a ball.

This fool of a demon. This absolute fool.

He had no ability to remember, so he forgot my orders the moment I gave them.

Argh... That Sacred Treasure, at least, I had to get back. Everything had been going so well for so long that I got lax, let my guard down.

I pushed too hard. I should never have tried to go straight for the prince's body.

That was my chance: switch bodies with a prince who was engaged to marry Lalatina, and I would obtain everything I had always wanted. I leaped at the chance, at the opportunity to get all of it at once, and as a result, some thief stole my Sacred Treasure and now here I was.

If I'd given it directly to the prince, I would only have had to recite the incantation and then destroy this body for all of it to be mine. I couldn't stop cursing myself, but now the first thing was to find out where the item went.

Sigh... If I'd known things were going to turn out this way, I wouldn't have waited around. I would have just switched bodies with my son, Balter, and been done with it...

If I don't get that item back, there will have been no point to my bothering to take *him* in. I worked hard to find an intelligent child with a bright future. If only he could have successfully concluded the betrothal to Lalatina, I wouldn't have had to go to such dangerous lengths...

"Lalatina! Lalatina! You are mine, Lalatina! Do you know how long I've watched you?!" I shouted into the dim basement, letting my anger at having lost the item carry me away.

The disturbing demon began to get excited. "*Wheeze! Wheeze!*

You're wonderful, Alderp! Ever loyal to your appetites, twisted and cruel—I like you very much, Alderp! I want to grant your wish quickly, Alderp; I want to receive my reward! Now set me to work, Alderp! Tell me what you wish, Alderp! Alderp!"

Truly worthless. Even if he granted my wish, he'd immediately forget he did so. If it weren't so easy to bilk him on his reward, I would summon some other monster.

I held a round stone in my hand. A Sacred Treasure that allowed me to summon and control a random monster. I caressed the stone.

"I have only one wish! Bring me Lalatina! She belongs to me!"

How many times had I told him what my wish was? I had lost track. But now, I told him once again.

As the magic circle from Lain's Teleport spell vanished, the room turned quiet. I couldn't believe what a difference there was with and without those people.

I stared at the spot where the magic circle had been. "Your Highness," Claire said, "please don't...don't be too upset."

She went on. "I admit that since that man came, you truly seemed to be enjoying yourself; you seemed truly happy. But that man... He's from another world. If you became too attached to a particular member of the opposite sex, it would only be painful for both of you when you were finally married, as princess. I will accept your rebuke. But please understand why it had to be this way..."

Claire closed her eyes and bowed her head deeply. Beside her, Lain, too, was looking at the floor.

"I'm all right. Please, both of you, look at me."

The two women slowly raised their heads. The pained looks they both wore told me of their care for me, as well as their resolve.

I felt no resentment toward them. I didn't even see a need for such a feeling.

I stretched out my left hand, looking at my fingers. One spot on my ring finger was lighter than the rest of my skin. The ring that had been there for so long had kept it from getting tanned.

The sight of me staring at my empty finger seemed to trigger some guilt in Claire and Lain, because they burst out:

"I-I'm very sorry! We lacked the strength to keep you from losing your precious ring...!"

"Whatever can we do to make up for this failure...?!"

I wasn't exactly unhappy about the loss.

"Both of you did your best. A number of capable adventurers were staying in the castle that night, so I suspect the ring would have been stolen no matter who was in command. I'll talk to my father when he gets home to ensure there's no need to place blame. So please don't look so distraught."

Claire was making herself smaller and smaller as I spoke. She was very talented, but she did tend to be too serious. I was hoping she might relax a little after working with *him* for a while. The way Lalatina had.

"I'm very grateful to hear you say that. You've not only lost your ring but had to part with that man... Your Highness. If he should defeat another of the Demon King's generals, you'll see him again..." Claire looked apologetic as she tried to comfort me.

Defeat one of the Demon King's generals. That was no simple task, but I was sure he could do it, if anyone could. And I was sure he wouldn't wait around.

"You're right. I'm sure we'll see him again soon," I said with a smile.

Claire frowned with displeasure.

Cheerfully, as if to encourage me, Lain said, "Seeing you recently, milady, I expected you would say something selfish when Master Kazuma left us... But you certainly defied those expectations! I worried Master Kazuma had been a bad influence on you, but I see I shouldn't have." Her words brightened the mood.

"That's because Elder Brother promised me," I said with a smile.

"Promised you...? Ahh, you mean about finishing your game. Beat the pants off him, Your Highness!" Claire said. But that wasn't the promise I had in mind.

*   *   *

Since time immemorial, it had been said in this country that the hero who defeated the Demon King would be given the right to marry the princess as a reward.

I looked again at the spot where my ring had been and whispered, so the two of them couldn't hear me: "I hope you'll take care of my ring, Big Brother."

Epilogue 2 — Instead of a Dream, I Got a Ring

When we returned to Axel, courtesy of Lain's Teleport spell...

"Ahhhhhhhhhhhhhhhhhhhhhhhhhhhh!"

We headed back to our mansion, where I threw myself down on the sofa and flung my arms and legs around like a child mid-tantrum.

Darkness glanced at me, then sat down and took a sip of tea. "Hey, can it. You're a nuisance to the whole neighborhood. If you need to scream that loudly, go out of town to do it."

"Get off my back, you dumb jerk! You ruined everything! If you hadn't brought up the Demon King, I'm sure Iris would have made a different wish! 'I want to stay with Elder Brother,' or 'I want to date Elder Brother,' or 'I want to sleep with Elder Brother' or something!"

"Careful what you say! Don't forget that Princess Iris is only twelve years old! She was never going to say any of those things anyway, not there! Maybe she might have said something like, 'Let's hire him on as the royal jester.' Anyway, you hardly lived with her for more than a week, right? Do you have enough confidence to become this attached to a member of the opposite sex in such a short time? Face reality... Come on, I'll make you some tea, so calm down."

"Don't talk to me about reality! I've been in a dream, living with a princess! I don't want your logic or your arguments. I only just left her—let me dream a little longer!"

Megumin sat down next to me with only a sidelong glance at our argument.

"And Megumin!" I said. "I know how short-tempered you are, but how could you start a fight right at the last minute?!"

"Oh, that was a fight we had to have, as two little-sister types do. Not to mention that when we went out into the capital together, I very nearly got her into an excellent fight. In the end we weren't able to rough up those punks together, so it was sort of a parting gift from me."

I wanted to point out that she was the jailbait type, not the little-sister type, or tell her not to teach the princess weird things like that, but I saw that before I had realized what was happening, Megumin had become good friends with Iris, too. Maybe their friendship had blossomed because their ages were so close, and maybe they had been trying to put on a brave front for each other when Megumin had to leave.

Darkness gave me the tea she had prepared, while Megumin took out a piece of paper and began assiduously writing something on it. I peeked over her shoulder: It looked like a letter to someone. Iris, I'll bet. I sipped my tea and grinned to myself as I realized Megumin had a more laid-back side, as well.

Aqua bustled out of the kitchen with a glass, which she set on the table along with the bottle of wine she had been clutching all this time. Then she sat on the sofa.

"Megumin, what are you writing?" she asked. "I get it—you're going to send a letter to the princess, aren't you? I remember you two talking in a room after the party ended yesterday. You were on a first-name basis and everything."

Megumin went on scratching away at the paper, her face serious. "You're wrong. This is a fan letter. I want to make sure it's ready so I can give it to that masked thief anytime I might meet him."

Darkness and I both spit out our mouthfuls of tea.

"*Cough! H-hack!* M-Megumin, do you like that notorious masked thief that much? Are you sure 'fan letter' is the right term for what you're writing? This person is a criminal, remember." Apparently, Darkness didn't intend to give away that I was the thief.

"Like him? In a way, I suppose. In this day and age, there aren't many people who are so dramatic. Even by Crimson Magic Clan standards, someone so unusual is, well, rather unusual. And he managed to break in to the castle with just one accomplice, and they were unstoppable. Don't you want to root for him? I'm not so much in love with him as a man—it's more a kind of hero worship."

...Now what? Revealing my identity seems a bit less attractive now.

Then we heard a dry, popping sound, and a lovely fragrance filled our living room. Aqua must have opened the wine.

"Hey, that smells good. Give me some," I said.

"Say the magic words. Say, 'Lady Aqua, please be so kind as to share some of your wine.'"

...Forget it. I'll just steal it.

I stood up to take the bottle, but Aqua quickly closed the top, put it back in her bag, and hunkered down like a turtle.

"Hey, don't fight me for it! Just hand it over!"

"No way! Stop it—let me have this! Please, I'll do anything, but just let me have this one thing!"

Any outsider who happened to see us might assume I was doing something practically inhuman to Aqua. She had curled up into a ball, and I was shaking her shoulders.

Darkness, her face red, was hitting my shoulders and wriggling her lower body.

"Me too… I'll even pay you; just let me in on this role-play…"

"It's not role-play! You were actually pretty cool in the capital a couple of times; where did that Darkness go? …Sheesh. Hey, Aqua!"

She obviously wasn't going to budge, so I tried to compromise.

"I'll go buy you some delicious wine from that guy Michael or whoever right now. Then we'll wager our bottles on a contest. You managed to be a little bit helpful this time in spite of yourself, so as a reward, I'll take a handicap."

At this, Aqua reluctantly looked up, checking to see if I was serious.

"...Really? You'd go out to buy some wine just so you can have a contest with me? That's really something. Are you sure there isn't a catch?"

I guess she did learn something once in a while.

But I had her right where I wanted her. One more push would do it. I just needed to think of a convincing reason.

"Well, I mean, again, it was in spite of yourself, but you did kind of help save the capital. And we're all home safe and sound, and I just wanted to celebrate that. There's obviously not enough wine there for three people anyway."

"Wait just a second, are you not counting me because you once again intend to make me drink juice? And what do you mean, safe and sound? Weren't you murdered by kobolds?"

"K-keep it to yourself! I'm alive now, aren't I? Safe is safe! Anyway, you're too young to drink. I'll buy you a nice cold Neroid, and you can just wait until you're old enough for anything else."

When I brought up her age, Megumin slammed the half-written letter down on the table.

"I am old enough to get married! I can handle a little wine! I challenge you to a drinking contest!"

That's an alternate world for you. Wow, is Megumin really old enough to get married?

"H-hey, look, I don't think alcohol would be good for you," Darkness said. "But I guess we are celebrating. And we did stop an uncouth villain from succeeding in his dastardly plans. Okay, I'll make something to go with our drinks. We're finally home. I guess we can afford to have a feast this one night." She stood and went to the kitchen.

Aqua perked up immediately on hearing the word *feast*. "Look, Kazuma, you haven't been back in nearly a week. We don't need to have a contest or anything. I think I could see my way to sharing with everyone else. Just a little bit."

She set the bottle back on the table. I thought about pointing out that she had dodged a bullet, but I didn't want to spoil the mood. I had gotten the little sister I'd always wanted—even if I'd had to leave her again after just a short while. I could be congenial for one day.

"I'm off to buy wine, then. If I let Kazuma go, I suspect I'll find myself stuck with a Neroid!" Megumin announced, then flew out the door.

A little while later, the smell of something cooking drifted in from the kitchen.

"So we have wine and a snack," Aqua said. "All we need for a real banquet now is a party trick…"

All of this felt so normal. It almost made me think my time in the capital really had been just a dream. Had I actually lived with a princess? Had she really called me Elder Brother and looked up to me? I took out the ring, the proof that I hadn't just dreamed it, and stared at it wistfully…

At just that moment, Aqua, looking for something to use in her trick, spotted it.

"Oh! Hey, Kazuma, lend me that ring, will you? I'll show you the most amazing magic trick!"

I admit I was a little curious, but I knew what happened to the rings she used in her tricks.

Aqua reached out for the ring, but I put it away before she could grab it…!

Afterword

Hello, everyone, it's your singing, dancing author, Natsume Akatsuki.

I've decided to work on my body so I'll be ready anytime I might get sent to another world. I've heard that ramping up the exercise too quickly is actually bad for you, so I've started by doing some light calisthenics and reading a lot of fighting manga. If you don't see me next volume, you'll know I was either summoned to another world or became a grappler.

...Enough rambling. I'll use this space to tell you what's coming up with *Konosuba* instead.

Simultaneous with the release of this volume, TORANOANA will be releasing a drama CD. The script is based on one of my short stories—pick it up if you want to catch an adventure that can only be heard on this CD.

Incidentally, the first volume of the manga version by Masahito Watari is coming out next month. Please look forward to Kazuma and his adventures as they can only be seen in comics.

By the way, I signed some papers for the *Isekai* Fair the other day. I never thought in all my life I would actually autograph something, so I practiced and practiced, got some extra paper in case I screwed it up, and was all prepared—and then the things my editor sent me had an illustration on them.

So all my preparations went to waste, and I signed the illustrated papers with a trembling hand, thinking, *I must not fail.* Next time someone asks me to autograph something, I think I'm going to cry and fight them about it.

Now, then.

We have here another volume in which I extend my gratitude to Kurone Mishima-sensei, along with my editor and designer, my proofreader, and the entire editorial staff, and all the people who helped get this book published.

In what seems like the blink of an eye, I realize I'm in my second year as an author. I'll keep on writing, and I hope you'll keep on reading!

More than anything else, my deepest thanks go to all the readers of this book. Thank you!

Natsume Akatsuki

This is bad! This is so, so bad!

What is it? I'm still torn up about Iris.
If it's dangerous, count me out.

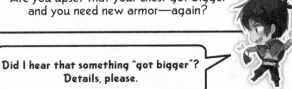

You're usually so calm, Darkness.
Are you upset that your chest got bigger
and you need new armor—again?

Did I hear that something "got bigger"?
Details, please.

Is it that tentacled monster you've always wanted?
Maybe she got a magically altered Roper.

Wait, what got bigger, exactly?
And tell me about this Roper...

You're both wrong! But I might...
I might get married! For real this time!

...CONGRATULATIONS?

?!

COMING SOON!!

KONOSUBA: GOD'S BLESSING ON THIS WONDERFUL WORLD! 7

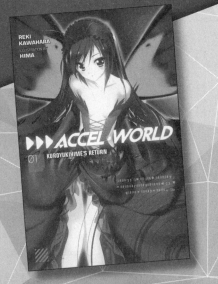

PRESS "SNOOZE" TO BEGIN.

DEATH MARCH TO THE PARALLEL WORLD RHAPSODY

After a long night, programmer Suzuki nods off and finds himself having a surprisingly vivid dream about the RPG he's working on...only thing is, he can't seem to wake up.

MANGA

LIGHT NOVEL